The Siberian's Queen

A.J. Wynter

Copyright © 2017 A.J. Wynter

All rights reserved.

ISBN: 1542370884
ISBN-13: 978-1542370882

DEDICATION

To the man who inspired the dark tiger.

1.

Katerina tugged the thick arctic fox blanket over her eyes hoping to block out the sun that had so rudely awakened her. She didn't want to get up because getting up meant facing her parents, and discussing the meeting of her soon to be husband, Sergei.

She groaned into her pillow; she didn't want an arranged life! All Kat had ever wanted was to be young and free. She dreamt of roaming the Russian woods and living off the land like a nomad. Or maybe she would head south and be a water nomad, fishing for sustenance on a daily basis. She would live near the sea, lounging in a hammock she had woven with her own hands.

Her wealthy parents just scoffed at her wild young imagination, seeing no value in Katerina being a strong and self-reliant young woman. They lectured her about preparing for life as a Princess, and how to take care of a husband. Katerina, or Kat as she preferred, was part of the royal Emerald family, also known as the wealthiest family in North Eastern Russia. At least a hundred aunts, uncles, cousins, grandparents, and offspring extended their reach and control all over the country. They traveled in smooth black limousines, had huge entourages, and never went anywhere by foot, save for their expansive courtyards.

Kat crawled out of bed and let her staff bathe and dress her in a simple cotton shirtdress. She planned to spend the day holed up in the cedar hedges by the pool, reading.

As a child, growing up in an estate so large, she learned that she could hide in multitudes of places and her mother would never find her. She would spend this stolen time enveloped in books about adventurers and imagining travelling and living a gypsy life.

After hours of exploring the grounds and reading, Kat stood up and shoved her dirty feet into her shoes and tried to brush the dirt off her dress.

When she trudged back into the lavish palace, her mother grilled her, like she always did.

"Where were you all afternoon? Don't tell me you were off gallivanting with the next-door neighbors."

"Mama, we don't have next-door neighbors unless you count Francesca and she's three miles down the road."

Her mother shook her head and walked away. Kat watched her Mother's tiny frame march off irritated, perched atop 4" stilettos. She and her Mother were both exactly five feet tall with long blonde hair. Her mother preferred to have her staff tie her own back in a bun or to keep it in a fancy updo, but Kat always wore hers loose and wild. It pleased her to feel the wind whip her hair around her face as she ran through the gardens in the summer. She loved the ice that would form on her strands from her breath in the winter, like strands of crystals or diamonds. They looked almost like sisters, but that's where the similarities ended.

Kat didn't care about traditional beauty, or learning how to run a vast household. Kat also didn't care about her arranged marriage.

Her mind drifted back to her daydream about being a sea nomad. She would meet a tall, dark, handsome prince whom she would fall madly in love with. His name wouldn't matter, nor would his legacy. Kat imagined him arriving draped in furs, his dark hair flopping lazily into his icy blue eyes. He would have a dark steed to match, or perhaps a pure white one? She was undecided about the minutiae but the main character always remained the same.

"Who are you?" Kat would ask dismissively. "Leave me be; this is my sacred place."

"I've been watching you for a long time, Miss Emerald. You are the most beautiful girl and I must have you as mine," he'd reply dramatically and with flourish.

She would pause equally dramatically, "why should I go with you, what can you offer a woman like me?" He would leap off his horse, grab her around the waist, snake his gloved hand through her hair and kiss her hard and passionately. She would faint into his arms and he would lift her onto his majestic steed and—

"Kat? Kat! Hello? I don't believe it. What is wrong with this child? For years, we prayed for you to turn into a proper heiress and look at what we ended up with. A lazy tomboy that has gotten dirt stains on her dress! Get upstairs and get in the bath! You've ruined your clothes."

Kat looked up at her father, who had also just come in from touring the grounds. "Hi Papa," she said.

"Hello, darling. I hear your mother is a touch angry with you."

Kat felt at ease around her father. He was a kind and reasonable man, and only wanted the best for her.

His marriage to Natalia had been quite scandalous; he was a poor boy from a farming village out west, whereas her mother was a rich landowner's daughter of the East. They'd met while her Mother's family were on a trading trip and had fallen in love. Their love story sounded like one out of the movies; one of the cars the Emerald family had been traveling in had driven over a nail in the road, completely deflating the tire. It was fortuitous her father was there; he had been herding cows across a dirt path when he stumbled across the Emerald's crippled entourage and was able to patch the tire with supplies from his wagon. Completely smitten with her beauty and elegance, he vowed to pursue her family's acceptance for marriage.

Of course, the Emerald family was not happy with Natalia's choice. She was practically disowned because of their love affair. His acceptance was hard fought, and Kat thought it was the most romantic story in the world. This was precisely why she didn't want an arranged marriage. There just wasn't enough love in it for her; let alone passion.

She often wondered if her mother regretted her choice as she certainly wasn't letting Kat choose her own suitor. Kat thought it was extremely hypocritical of her.

Kat realize that she had forgotten her book in the cedar hedge and stole out into the courtyard in her bare feet to find it. As she ran, something bright flashed in her peripheral vision. It was a swift and fast movement, and when looked back again, she saw the cedar hedge branches had been disturbed, but nothing was there.

She picked up her speed again, not wanting to make her mother any angrier than she already was. When she rounded the corner, she stopped dead in her tracks. Ahead, staring intently at her, was a huge Siberian tiger.

Kat backed gingerly away, heart pumping in her chest. The tiger simply sat down and watched her retreat. She was afraid at first, but something about the tiger's demeanor made her feel like she could trust it.

She turned and walked calmly the whole walk back to the manse. If she announced the presence of a tiger, the guards would be alerted. They would take after it with guns blasting, shooting it dead before the poor beast returned to the forest.

Kat was an ardent animal lover. She had given up eating meat years earlier and felt terribly guilty about the abundance of furs in the palace. She justified using the furs, as the animals had already been killed and didn't want their death to be totally for naught. Her mother justified their use as a way to keep the economy of the far north thriving.

Once at the palace stairway, Kat searched the shrubbery and spotted the cat's golden eyes swiveling back and forth, following her every move. Kat was safe from it, for now. Kat hastened through the massive ornately carved front door.

.

2

The tigers' human name was Daman. He had lived in Mongolia for most of his life, but had migrated back to Russia when a forest fire had eradicated his habitat. He'd lost his mother and brother in that fire; the pain of their deaths had left him devastated and alone. He grew cold and calloused as a way to protect his heart, and vowed he would never feel so deeply again. That was until he caught sight of Kat.

He was an animorph, a man who could change from human to beast without the assistance of a full moon; in his instance, a tiger. He was tall with tanned skin and golden eyes. His hair was thick and black with slight highlights of red and orange. In his Siberian tiger form, Daman was almost four hundred pounds of muscle and meat. He could take down any prey or adversary, and was one of the best hunters around for hundreds of miles. Locally he had befriended a Siberian or two but most of the others avoided him. They knew he was a migrant, but knew little else. It was better this way; letting anyone in was too dangerous. They could hurt you, or worse, die because of you.

But Kat was different someh...

No! Daman thought to himself. *Did you see all those guards standing around the palace grounds? They would kill you in an instant. All it would take is one bullet to the head, and you would be another rug on their floor. Stop thinking about her!* He made a half-hearted effort to dismiss her from his thoughts.

If only he could. He couldn't stop thinking about the girl with the emerald eyes and the white sundress, with hair so long and golden that it reached far below her waist. He noticed her porcelain skin was luminescent, opalescent even, and that she enjoyed basking in the sun, making friends with butterflies. Daman had taken to stalking her these past few months. He observed that she ate her veggies on the porch every day, with an enormous book spread out in front of her. Was it a bible? No, it was something else, an atlas! In all his travels, he had never come across such an intriguing young woman.

It was on bright summer days like these, watching this fascinating young woman, Daman could feel his cold heart beginning to thaw. He turned briskly on his paw and bounded back into the forest. It wasn't safe to remain after Kat had left. He instinctively knew that she would save him from sudden death if he was discovered. One word from her, and the guards would drop their guns. But with her absence, the guards were a constant looming threat.

As Daman retreated, he began to recall the ancient tales about a time before humans; a time when Daman had yet been born, and his kind still roamed the earth in large numbers. They populated the molten earth, sabre-toothed and strong, hunting and living in streaks.

Of course, Daman could travel in a streak if he wanted to. There were other tigers that would surely run and hunt with him. But he loved and craved solitude. He was a rogue tiger, rugged and strong, and he answered to no one. When in human form, he squatted in an abandoned apartment building in the closest town. Daman didn't have any record of his birth, and trying to fit into an ordinary life proved too difficult. But who was he kidding? He enjoyed living like a vagabond. He spent his days hunting and his nights partying at nightclubs and raves. There he could find plenty of eager volunteers to feed his primal sexual hunger; which, because of the tiger blood running through him, were much higher than a normal man. But his heart remained closed.

Enough. Stop thinking about her and do something else. It's not worth it, she's not worth it. She's just another entitled princess. I bet she eats meat in secret.

He crawled into his apartment, ready for his midday nap. The moment he reached the top floor, he collapsed onto his mattress on the floor. Daman fell asleep in the light of the mid-afternoon sun beaming through his window, waking hours later to the call of the wild. It had become his pattern.

By the time he left his apartment the sky was jet black. The heat of high summer had finally broken, the temperature dropping to an easy 73 degrees. Daman raced down the broken apartment steps, his heart pounding in his chest. He was starving for a woman, and if he wasn't careful, would kill the next living being that crossed his path. Daman slammed out the back door and ran onto the main road. The streets were empty for the most part; the only people outside were a young couple smoking cigarettes.

Even though this was the richer part of the country, the city's exterior walls gave off the impression that it was falling apart. While the inside of every building was well furnished, covered in glistening polished floors and thick, dark Oriental rugs, the outsides were crumbling and barred up. There were often crystal chandeliers hidden towards the back, away from the windows and away from the prying eyes of the beggars. If Daman had the money, he would live in secrecy, just like the guilty rich. His carpet would be dark green, like his favorite forest leaves. Maybe the chandelier would also be green, or emerald...

Emerald.

Again, his mind went back to Kat: Kat, with her glittering green eyes, and her flowing blonde hair. In another world, if he had money, they could be together.

But we can never be together. We come from two very different worlds. I need a fucking drink.

Exasperation quelled his hunger. He smiled to himself and slicked his hair back. It would definitely take his mind off everything to go have a drink at a club, the very place to find a 'distraction'. His favorite was an underground club in an abandoned railroad site called 'Broken Glass'. It was accessible through an abandoned subway entrance and kept camouflaged with thick vines throughout the summer.

Daman rushed down the stairs, excited for the possibility of quenching the slow fire in him, with liquor and a woman. The minute his body was underground, he felt the strong bass pulsing through his body. The neon lights bounced off the walls and an enormous disco ball dangled from the ceiling. The club was packed with people wearing masks. On nights like this, when he found himself stuck thinking about the loss of his family and the impossibility which was Kat, Daman preferred to be around other human beings; it soothed that human part of him. He drew comfort when they pushed up against him, and even smiled when they accidentally stepped on his toes. An innocent physical contact to help fill the hole he had in him. And he had no qualms about taking a woman home and fucking her, without any exchanging of names, for exactly the same reason.

It was a strange existence, being alone and also a shifter. The differing needs of both sides of him were often in conflict.

The bar area was tucked inside an abandoned train car. He swayed towards the bartender, and debated between ordering a beer or something harder. He noticed a girl standing in the corner of the bar, wearing an orange and black mask over her eyes. A tigress, aloof and on the hunt. She stood with her back pressed against the wall as any good hunter would. Daman glanced at her, and she flashed her eyes at him from behind the mask.

"Vodka. Rocks," he grunted to the bartender, who nodded. He handed Daman a glass filled to the brim; the bartender knew what he expected.

When he turned to look at the mystery girl, she was gone. Certain that she was equally stunning beneath her tiger mask, the booze started to relax him and the thought of the woman make him feel a tightness in the groin. He needed to find her. Though it had been easy to navigate the crowd the first time around, the crush of so many others hiding from their real lives impeded his progress. People were no longer moving aside for him; in fact, it felt as if they were moving closer together. He took a deep breath, and felt like he was suffocating. The crowd was closing in on him, pressing into him like the weight of the ocean when he dove too deeply. Too much! Too many! If this kept up, he would surely suffocate out on the dance floor.

He was having a panic attack. They didn't happen often, or at least not anymore, but they'd started after the death of his family. It was difficult for him to calm himself down when he was like this. It usually took a lot of deep breaths and a long bath in the arms of a woman, or alternatively, the easy fix of a Xanax. Tonight he had none of that; the enormity of how alone he was hitting him hard

Earlier that evening one of the palace guards, a young boy named Jaime, had told Kat about the party. He'd propositioned Kat on more than one occasion but she turned him down every time; this party invitation was obviously another attempt. She secretly admired his tenacity, so she agreed to accompany him to the party. It was against the rules to leave the grounds after sundown, but Kat picked and chose which rules she felt like following on any particular day. Besides, the anonymity afforded her by being masked gave her that extra security. She needed the distraction.

She scanned the room, focusing as hard as she could on the eyes behind the masks for any sign of Jaime or anyone else that she knew. All around her, the music was pumping and the alcohol coursing through her body made her feel dizzy. She liked it. She could feel the tension of her restrictive life leaving her body.

Across the way, Kat saw the man whose eyes had met hers, crouching against the wall with his head in his hands. Unlike everyone else, had arrived without a mask.

She stepped towards the man on the floor.

"Hey," she shouted, extending a slender hand. "Are you alright?"

He looked up at her through enormous golden-brown eyes. Thick strands of hair had fallen in front of his eyes. They weren't the green eyes of the man in her fantasy, but they took her breath away.

"Hi," he mouthed. He seemed as taken aback as she felt.

"What?"

"I said hi!" he shouted, trying to be heard over the music.

"Outside?" she shouted back and motioned to the vine covered entryway.

He nodded, standing up; but mid attempt, a drunk girl stumbled into him and knocked him back onto the ground.

"Oh!" Kat exclaimed, dropping to her knees. She helped the stranger to his feet, wrapping a slender arm around his waist.

'Hmmmph. I always thought this would be the other way around. Are all Russian men this frail?" she thought. He certainly didn't *feel* frail. She could feel his taut body and sculpted muscles under his jacket. Confused, she helped him to his feet.

The mystery girl led him by the hand through the crowd. People seemed to make way for her, as if they knew who she was.

"Who are you?" he yelled over the pulsating music.

She smiled at him, and pretended she couldn't hear him. When they finally made it up the stairs, he breathed in the air and smiled. The night was now crisp and cool, and he gulped in all the breaths of fresh air he could.

"Finally, you're free," she said.

"Indeed, I am," he responded, gratefully.

"What happened in there?"

"I'm not sure, but I think that being in the large crowd overwhelmed me."

"I certainly get that. Are you alright now?"

"Yes, thank you for helping me. That certainly was embarrassing."

"Do you want to go for a walk?" Kat asked boldly.

"Sure. Where should we go? Is there someone you need to tell?"

"Actually, preferably somewhere no one will find us," she said, laughing.

"I know just the spot."

He took her hand and led her towards the only area on earth he felt safe: the forest.

Kat smiled at the warmth of his hand enveloping hers. She knew that this was dangerous, leaving with a stranger, but something in his eyes implored her to follow him wherever he went.

Daman also knew that leading a young girl into the forest was risky for many reasons. Her trust and naivety made him want to protect her even further. He was basically the king of this patch of land, and he made sure the other carnivores knew it. There was only one tiger who could challenge him. When they got to the edge of the trees, she hesitated.

"What's wrong?" he asked.

"Is it safe?"

"It is because I'm here. But you must never come here alone."

"Ah, another rule," she sighed.

"What?" he asked, scrunching up his face.

"Oh, it's nothing. Ready?"

He nodded.

"Well, lead the way."

The forest smelled fresh and crisp, and the aroma of pine needles filled the night air. Everywhere Kat walked there were patches of moss in all shades of green, as well of scourges of mosquitoes that seemed to gather around her legs.

"This is incredible," she breathed. "I've never seen anything like it in my entire life."

"What kind of life do you lead if you've never been in the forest?" he asked, not in a mocking way, but as if he genuinely couldn't believe it.

"Oh, I've been in lots of forests, just not this particular one," she lied.

They had walked fairly deep into the woods, but Daman took her deeper still. She saw a clearing up ahead, with a small lake glinting in the moonlight. The body of water was surrounded by tall, twisting trees covered in deep claw marks and tufts of fur from when Daman was in a playful mood. The beauty of the clearing in the moonlight made her gasp and smile.

"How did you find this place?" she asked in awe.

"This is where I go to eat breakfast, lunch and dinner."

She didn't respond, curious and intrigued by a man who packed a lunch to eat in the forest.

Kat realized she was still holding the man's hand. She squeezed it once for good measure. She'd never held the hand of someone of the opposite sex before, unless she counted her father, which she didn't. It was exhilarating to be out here with him. She'd always dreamed of getting away in nature, far from the palace and its guards, and exploring alone. Although she imagined going somewhere far away, she had no idea that this magic existed so close to home.

When they got to the clearing, she turned and met his gaze. The mask had started to get unbearably hot and impeded her vision. She didn't want to miss any of the beauty in front of her, so she slid the mask up on top of her head.

"This is incredible," she said, looking firmly into his eyes.

His eyes grew large, and his lips struggled to move. He gasped, "Kat..."

3

Natalia Emerald entered the hallway. Something in her gut had told her to check on her daughter. She had seemed so unsettled as of late. She approached Kat's closed bedroom door and made to knock, but lowered her hand deciding against it. She did not want to invade her daughters much guarded privacy, nor disturb her slumber. She shook off her feeling of unease.

Natalia turned and walked down the hall towards her room, past a window the size and length of a hallway. Peering out, she could see the garden in all of its splendor. There were iron floodlights highlighting a fountain filled with large Grecian sculptures. She lingered at the window but didn't notice the dark figure darting across the yard.

Once she returned to her chambers, she fell sound asleep. On multiple occasions she'd caught Kat sleeping in the outdoor hammock, and there was always a guard with his eyes glued to her. Tonight, she felt reassurance that her only daughter was safely inside the heavily guarded walls of the mansion. She could not have known that it was one of these hired men who was responsible for escorting her past the palace walls.

Kat and the golden-eyed man had walked home hand in hand from the forest, and he had finally introduced himself as Daman. She felt at ease with him the entire time they walked. When they reached the steep walls, he stopped and turned to face her. She could tell that he wanted to kiss her.

"Do you want to come inside one day? I'd love to show you around the garden, or the courtyard."

"I don't think that's a very good idea," he said. "And aren't there guards stationed all over the place? I'll be killed."

"You won't be killed, Daman. It's not like you're a wild animal or a vagrant. The only things I've seen the guards shoot are quails and other beasts, but never a human. At least I've never seen them shoot another human."

"That's troublesome," he mused.

When he looked at her, Kat felt something strange stirring within her chest. It felt like her ribcage had taken itself apart and exposed her heart. It was hard to breathe with him looking at her like that.

"What are you thinking about?" he asked, as he tucked a stray lock of hair behind her ear.

"Nothing," she lied. "What are you thinking about?"

He smirked and remained silent. She had a feeling she'd never get a word out of him but it was fun to ask anyway.

"Goodnight, Kat," he said, swooping low to kiss her on the cheek.

"When can I see you again?" she asked, with no hesitation.

"Soon. I'll come find you."

"But the guards—" she started to say, but before she could finish her sentence, Daman kicked off his shoes and pulled his shirt over his head before dropping to his hands and knees.

The sudden movement startled her, but what came next caused her to step back in total shock. His bronzed skin crawled and sprouted fur. He arched his neck back to the sky as his facial features morphed. His hands thickened, nails replaced with sharp black claws. Suddenly, a massive orange and black tiger appeared right before her eyes. His cat eyes stared at her intently while he emitted a low purr. He rubbed his body up against her legs then turned on his paw, and bounded off towards the forest.

She placed a hand to her chest and gasped; it had felt as though the entire evening she'd been holding her breath. Even if her mother caught her in the garden and she was punished, there was no way she would forget about the most magical and exalting experience of her life.

Glancing both ways, she emerged from a wiry cluster of trees and ran across the courtyard, carefully skirting the edges. There was no way the guards would see her, she knew every inch of the courtyard and how to get around them.

One of Kat's earliest memories was that of a palace attack by a small group of Mongolian raiders. Instead of giving her up to be kidnapped, raped, or worse, every single guard in the building fought hard in order to protect her. She trusted them implicitly, but knowing she could come and go when she needed gave her a sense of freedom. With her mind still whirring about her magical night, exhaustion finally overtook her and she slept.

4

When Kat woke up, she felt warm and alive. Her first thought was that the night before had been a dream, yet it felt too real. With the lucidness of morning, she realized it was impossible that Daman really had turned into a giant tiger before her eyes. It was likely a figment of her overactive imagination, or maybe someone slipped something into her drink at the club.

Her thoughts were interrupted as her handmaids and dressers burst into her room. They were scurrying around, tearing open drawers and closet doors, barking orders at Kat. She sat up in bed and stared at them confusedly before it dawned on her that this was the day; the day she was to meet her 'betrothed'. Who was this Sergei? He would arrive wearing regalia, probably bearing water lilies, which were her favorite flower. And he would say something like, "I've never met a vision as beautiful as you." She'd heard it all before, with the past suitors and it all felt disingenuous. She sighed and dutifully allowed them to get her ready.

Even though her favorite color was green, the maids had picked out a prim and proper violet velvet dress for her. They looked at each other quizzically as they brushed bits of twigs from her messy hair.

Overwhelmed by it all, Kat gasped, "I need some privacy."

"Must you go right now, miss?" the senior dresser asked.

"Yes. Now. Please let go of my hair," she insisted peevishly.

They did as they were told, letting Kat's thick blonde hair fall around her shoulders. It curled slightly at the ends, and was meant to be placed into a delicate bun. She wore her mother's glass bead earrings, which were a pretty lilac color. For all intents and purposes, she was a beautiful princess. All she needed on her arm was a powerful 'prince' to inherit the estate.

As she left the room and entered the hallway she was so deep in thought that she walked straight into a sturdy wall of a chest, covered in white and gold. It was, she could only assume, Sergei.

"Watch where you're going," he barked.

"Right back at you. What is that you're wearing, a tablecloth?"

"You're one to talk," he spat. "You look like a wilted old tulip."

"What are you doing in my private wing anyway? Couldn't wait to meet me in the reception hall?"

He chuckled and raised an eyebrow at her. "Not even close. I'm casing the property to come back later and get me some fancy silverware."

Part of her wanted to punch him in the face, but Kat instead found herself blushing at his extreme moxie. He was nothing like Daman, but maybe that was a good thing.

Kat and Sergei had literally crashed into each other in front of one of the massive windows overlooking the garden. As they stood there Kat glanced out the window. She gasped as she caught a glimpse of something lurking in the corner behind the shrubbery. A tiger. He was watching Kat and Sergei through the trees. She doubted he could see her looking back; can tigers see as good as they can in the daylight as they do at night? She made a mental note to do research about the rare Siberian when she had a few minutes alone to herself. And what was he doing here? She wished he hadn't taken such a risk. If he wasn't careful, he would be spotted by the guards and killed instantly.

"Cat got your tongue?" Sergei said wryly, disrupting the silence.

"No," she responded icily. In only the few seconds she'd known him this man had already gotten under her skin. But to be fair, he'd come in with the deck loaded against him.

"Then what are you looking at?" he asked, turning to look out the window. Her heart leapt into her throat. Would Sergei see Daman in those trees, blowing his cover? But when she glanced back, the tiger was gone.

"It's a beautiful garden," he said.

"Oh, so the silverware thief has some taste?"

"Who says I'm a thief?"

"You're the one that blatantly announced your intent to trespass," she said.

"Maybe I just plan to assess your dowry, m-lady."

She flushed at his impudence.

"Kat! Oh good, I see you two have finally met." Her Mother intruded, making them both step back a pace. "Sergei, won't you join us in the tearoom? Kat, you're looking a bit rumpled, do you want to go get refreshed before tea?"

Sergei smirked at her, prompting Kat to stick out her tongue at him. Thankfully her mother didn't notice. She wasn't sure what it was, but something about Sergei was bringing out the bratty child within her. As a grown woman, she'd never joked around with a man this freely, and it felt refreshing. Days at the palace were usually spent focusing on studying, both academics and social responsibility. She never had any time for fun, let alone flirtation.

Sergei, on the other hand, was lucky to be inside the palace walls at all. While it was true he was to be the sole inheritor to a huge fortune, no one really knew where his family had earned it. There were rumors he came from a long line of Siberian Royalty born and bred in the heart of the north. And he definitely was suitable.

Sergei stopped to admire his image in one of the ornate gilded mirrors in the long hallway. He looked like the ideal suitor for someone of Kat's "standing"; with thick wavy locks of black hair, full lips, his dark eyes framed by long eyelashes, he certainly looked the part of a prince. He stepped back and gazed intently out the window. His ears darted around the courtyard for any signs of the stray shifter his father had warmed him about. He needed to ensure that the rogue cat stayed far away from his future wife.

The only way to please his father was to travel to the Emerald keep, which is exactly what he had done. But now that he was here, he felt out of place. He didn't have the same kind of grooming as Kat. Of course he had the clothes to match his title, but his personality was clearly more that of an arrogant servant boy, than a gentile prince. He definitely wasn't high brow material. But Kat didn't need to know that.

The two of them followed Natalia to the reception room, which was formally stocked with the makings of a proper English tea.

"Wait here, the both of you, and try to be nice to each other." Natalia barked and hustled off to find her husband.

Once she was out of sigh, Kat turned and walked the other direction.

"Where are you going?" Sergei asked.

"Let's go for a tour and get to know each other," she murmured, subtly motioning him to follow.

She led him down a long marble hallway and into the more secluded part of the palace. It was uninhabited by the rest of her family, and they used it only for parties and balls.

"This place is incredible," he said, marveling at the sweeping ceilings and marble slab walls.

"It is, I suppose, although it's a bit cold for my taste."

"So… what are we doing here?" he asked, cocking an eyebrow at her.

"Don't get coy with me; we're here to play a game."

"A game?"

"How about I go and hide and you try to find me?"

"That sounds like a terrible idea."

Kat grinned at his cowardice, and turned on her heel and ran away. He certainly was bringing out the playful girl in her!

Thankful for a minute alone, Sergei adjusted his throbbing manhood and shivered at his own touch. He was so turned on by this bratty little heiress.

Kat knew the perfect hiding place. It was in the corner of a walk-in closet, filled with party decorations. There were huge mirrored ornaments, silk flowers, shiny chains, and flimsy curtains that were meant to filter light into shimmering crystals. There was even a life size porcelain tiger that her mother brought out on special occasions. She hurried in without turning on the light, as she knew the closet by heart. The one thing she didn't account for was a real tiger sitting next to the porcelain one.

She walked towards the back of the closet in the darkness and gasped as her hand brushed up against something furry. At first she thought it was likely just another decoration, maybe one of her mother's many fur coats. But when she touched it for a second time, she realized it was warm and breathing.

"What the hell?" she hissed.

"I'm so sorry," came Daman's voice. Her hand was now resting on bare skin. She stumbled back into a suit of armor, which clanged to the floor. It hadn't been a dream!

From down the hall, she heard Sergei shouting, "I hear you!"

"Stay still and shut up" Kat hissed at him. "Sergei can't find you here".

"I need to warn you about him" Daman whispered.

"Warn me about what? He's to be my husband."

"Your what?" he asked, but she didn't respond, only shushed him again. She allowed herself to relax against his body, and was slightly shocked when she heard a deep but restrained purr. She was reminded again of the previous night, and their magical evening running around in the forest. It was like living in a fairy-tale—only a dark and complicated one. She could hear Sergei's footsteps in the hallway, but he walked straight past the closet and around the corner.

"You're safe for now, but we need to talk about this Sergei."

"How do you know anything about him?"

"I can't explain it, I just know. That's why I snuck in here, to warn you."

"I can take care of myself you know."

"I'm sure you can, but you may need some help with this one." He continued whispering in a hushed voice as he pulled Kat closer to his nude body.

He too was thinking about the events of the previous evening, and the rush of adoration he'd felt running around with Kat. He had shown her his tiger form and she hadn't freaked out at all. And she hadn't thought twice when she'd realized it was him in the closet with her. Was his unique genetic makeup even an issue? How could she be so calm and collected after seeing him shift? He enjoyed the way her body felt, pressed against his. He felt a strong urge growing within him to protect this woman at all costs. The best way to keep her safe for now, was to remain hidden. He pulled back from her and slipped amongst the rich fabrics hanging at the back of the room.

Suddenly, the storage door swung open, and Sergei crashed in, fumbling around in the dark. He tripped on one of the oriental rugs, crashing down in a heap of swearing. Kat, in her shock, tried to distract him from seeing Daman and coughed loudly. Sergei's eyes looked past Kat, as though searching for something else in the room. He seemed to be smelling the air. Her heart sank as her pulse quickened. There was no way he could miss a naked man in the room.

"Is that a tiger? It's so ridiculous."

She looked over her shoulder franticly trying to conjure up an explanation, but Daman was nowhere to be seen. Indeed, Sergei was looking at the large porcelain tiger.

"It looks nothing like a real tiger. And look at how its fangs are painted on. Whoever did this did a terrible job."

"And you've seen tigers up close before?" Kat asked.

"Have you?" he replied, leaning in close to her, smelling her neck.

For an instant, Kat thought he was going to kiss her, but instead he nuzzled his face into the collar of her dress, inhaling her scent. When he looked up at her, she swore that she saw anger in his eyes.

"It's not safe for you in here, let's go," he said, grabbing her hand and pulling her from the closet.

They heard her mother calling from down the hall. She glanced from Sergei to the porcelain tiger. Though Daman was nowhere to be seen, she was sure he was still lurking somewhere in the back hidden amongst the rich fabrics.

She smiled blandly at Sergei, slightly agitated that he had found her. She wanted to spend more time with Daman, and hear what he had to say about Sergei. But if she was being completely honest with herself, she felt drawn to both Sergei and Daman. She hated to admit it, but she was attracted to both of them.

There was a dampness growing in her panties and she was unsure who to attribute the wetness to; or was it both? She felt a warmth she had never felt before, growing in her abdomen, where both men had pressed up against her.

And with that she let Sergei lead her by the hand and into the tea room.

5

When they entered the tea room, they found Natalia perched in a far corner, surrounded by maids. They were each fussing over her, ensuring she had every need fulfilled. She looked like a Queen from the Romanov era; with a prim and proper demeanor, and her hair styled in an outdated updo topped with a diamond tiara. Yet, somehow she managed to look beautiful and terrifying at the same time. Since she was a young girl, she had always thought of her mother as an ice queen, and today she certainly looked the part.

She was beautiful and warm in front of strangers, but could be incredibly cold and calloused when it came to Kat. There were whole days dedicated to learning how to walk properly, how to sit up straight, and how to hold a glass of tea. Whenever Kat screwed something up, her mother would rap her sharply on the knuckles with a light brown ruler. Though she used to cry over it when she was younger, Kat had grown used to it. She knew that if Sergei wasn't in the room, her mother would surely be slapping her right now for running off with the heir apparent.

Natalia dismissed her ladies, then motioned for Kat and Sergei to be seated. She launched into a diatribe about how important it was for Kat to carry on the Emerald legacy. But Kat tuned her out, stuck in a reverie. All she could think about was Daman hiding in the closet. How had he gotten in there? There were half a dozen floors in the manor, and how did he get past the guards?

Kat snapped back to the moment when her mother revealed her plans for an animal print themed wedding, complete with live exotic animals.

"We're going to have a tiger at the wedding?" Kat asked. "Mother, don't you think that's a little bit over the top?"

"No, I do not. If you had any sense of the importance and magnitude of these nuptials you would understand that this is how the Emerald family throws weddings. We are built on a foundation of wealth and the people expect lavish parties."

"Where did you find a tiger?"

"Dear, your father has some local connections."

"So where is this wedding tiger?"

"I'm not sure where they've got it chained up. But, trust me, if it misbehaves at the wedding, or rehearsal, I've given a standing order for the guards to shoot it."

"Mother, you can't just shoot a living creature like that" she shrieked.

Kat glanced over at Sergei, but he just shrugged. Why wasn't he saying anything? It was inhumane to bring wild animals to such an event, and then to shoot the for being themselves – disgusting. Why didn't he protest? She barely knew Daman, but she did know that he would never willingly hurt another creature unless for survival.

She felt disgusted with both Sergei and her mother. But as much as Kat wanted to leave the tea room, she knew it would disappoint her mother. Once the awkward teatime was over, she politely excused herself under the guise of a headache, and withdrew to her bedroom. She felt like two women, each at odds with the other. The bold Kat told her to find Daman and run away with him, while the other, more practical girl told her to give Sergei a change. After all, she had familial obligations to fulfil, and Sergei was to be her future.

The minute her head hit the pillow, she burst into tears of frustration. Her tears were interrupted by a strange rustling coming from inside her closet. The rustling got louder, and the door slid open. It was Daman, still naked and in human form, with his beautiful golden eyes and dark chest hair. She was careful to avoid staring at anything below his navel; she was still a lady, and a virgin at that.

"What are you doing in here?" she whispered, wiping away tears.

"I've been evading your guards for hours now!"

"How did you know that this was my room?"

"I can smell you in here. It smells a whole lot better than that party room. What kind of garish parties are you throwing here?"

Kat giggled, "my mother has a thing for masquerade balls."

"Fancy, do you have a lot of these dress-up parties?"

"Actually, we do. My mother hosts them all the time. She's obsessed with flaunting her status. It can be pretty ridiculous at times."

He nodded, as if he understood. "So, Sergei is gone?"

"Yes, he's gone for now. Do you two know each other or something?"

"You could say that."

"What are you hiding from me?" she sighed, curious as to how the two men could possibly know each other; they were from entirely different worlds.

"I'll explain everything in due time. For now, you have to help me get out of here."

He walked towards her slowly, stopping when they were mere inches apart, and brushed her last tear away, "I hope everything is better now. No more tears."

She looked up into his deep gold eyes, a wave of emotion rushing over her.

"Can I see you again?"

"Of course."

"I'll sneak out later. I'll meet you on the edge of the garden."

She held his hands tightly, as if the tighter she held him, the longer he would stay. She noticed that Daman's eyes weren't just gold—they were flecked with shades of orange and brown. They reminded Kat of the 'Tiger's Eye' stone. She used to collect them when she was younger, stringing them on necklaces and making them into earrings. She'd stopped making her own jewelry when she grew older, especially when she started receiving jewelry from other suitors. They gave her dangling earrings and rings as fat as swollen knuckles. There were necklaces studded with sapphires and rubies, and then there were the emeralds.

She had bracelets, necklaces, rings –a huge trove of jewelry, each one studded with an emerald. They were meant to signify her legacy and her future, but when Kat looked at them, she just thought of them as a burden. They were the heavy stones that would drag her beneath the ocean of responsibility, sinking her, if she let them. Each piece of emerald jewelry was a cross to bear. There had been twenty-seven suitors in total; twenty-seven men who had marched in and out of the manor, and in and out of her life. None of them had stayed for too long. It had started when she was eighteen, and hadn't stopped since. She was now almost twenty-one years old, and still hadn't found a man she felt comfortable marrying. But now it seemed she was out of time, and suitors.

Why wouldn't her parents let her marry for true love? Her mother had. Interestingly enough, her father had allowed Kat to say no to all of the previous suitors, likely because he hadn't come from royalty himself. He had been introduced to this life through his marriage to Natalia, and he hadn't grown up with the same set of rules and standards that were now being forced on Kat. He didn't seem to care who Kat ended up marrying, but was pushing Sergei for some reason.

They slipped out of her room, peering both ways down the hall before running to the front door. Hardly anyone ever traveled to the front of the palace, and Daman had a better chance of escaping that way. Only six staircases stood between Daman and his freedom.

For him, he'd always known what it felt like to be free. He could come and go as he pleased, and he didn't have to stay in one place for too long.

But Kat, she's the heiress to a fortune and a legacy. Is it possible for her to live a life free of glamor and obligation? he wondered as they slunk through the expansive hallways.

"Tonight at twelve?" she asked, grabbing his hand just before he slipped out the massive front door.

He sighed and held her hand. "I'm sorry. I can't"

"What could've come up in the last five minutes?" she whispered sadly.

Daman hated having to reject her, but it was for the best. He had had a long time to think while stuck in the closet. Despite the longing he felt for her, Kat needed to forget about him. She would have a better future with Sergei, even though he was dangerous. Kat needed a suitor approved by her parents.

"Goodbye, Kat," he said, looking into her eyes one last time, before bounding off across the lawn and into the woods.

"Goodbye," she whispered, tears spilling over her eyelashes.

Kat spent the rest of the evening wracking her mind and analyzing those last few minutes with Daman. What could she have possibly done wrong? She must have done *something* to make Daman bolt like that. Were her tears too much?

Another more mortifying thought came to her mind. He was a tiger shifter. What if he could smell the desire on her and he didn't want her the same way?

Kat never felt badly about lying to her mother, but she did feel a little bit of guilt that she'd lied to Sergei about having a headache.

Kat was new to rejection. At first, she wallowed in sadness that Daman had left and turned her down. Then she got angry. She was a princess. She needed a prince with a backbone. Her thoughts quickly swung back to the arrogant suitor she had sent away.

6

"Mother, I'm going for a swim."

"Yes, but take Sergei with you. I don't want you swimming by yourself, especially when your father and I are out."

Kat's jaw dropped.

"Sergei? He's still here?"

"Of course he is. And he will remain here in the palace for the next month while we prepare for the wedding."

Excusing herself so quickly clearly wasn't seen as a rejection of him.

"What room is he staying in?" she asked, curiously.

"For heaven's sake Katerina, have you forgotten everything already? We always put the suitors in the reading wing."

Her mother stepped closer and placed a warm hand on her forehead. "Do you have a fever? Maybe you shouldn't be swimming."

"I'm fine, Mama. I'll go ask Sergei to be my lifeguard. When are you and Papa going to be back?"

"After the sun goes down. We've got to meet with someone from the military, an old friend of your father's. It might go pretty late, but I already gave the cook your dinner order."

She kissed her daughter on the forehead before sashaying down the hall. Her mother was regal and Kat had always found her walk so pompous. Kat tried mimicking her mother's footsteps, swaying her hips from side to side. She was so focused on her mockery of her mother that she didn't notice Sergei watching with a bemused look on his face.

"You look like a penguin," he said, startling her. She yelped and practically jumped out of her skin. She turned and smacked him in the chest.

"You're so rude!" she exclaimed.

"I'm rude? You aren't exactly the nicest host I've ever met, if you know what I mean," he said.

She scoffed. "Well, I don't have to be nice to you if I don't want to. I'm sure there are plenty of other suitors out there who would jump at the chance to marry me."

"Not likely, princess. I'm your last resort. Everyone knows that your mother is all out of options after me. She's trying not to act like it's a big deal, but if we don't get married, then the Emerald legacy is in trouble."

"What are you talking about? You're lying," she bemoaned.

"Of course she kept this from you. You're her only daughter! She probably wanted to keep you safe from this news. Why do you think she's going out tonight?"

"They're meeting my father's friend. He works for the military."

"Right. They're meeting to try and figure out your options. She needs to know if the laws of the land allow you to inherit without a man by your side. We still have some pretty primitive rules when it comes to the inheritance of such large parcels of land and property. If you ask me, I'd say it's risky."

Kat shook her head, feeling overcome by chills. "I can't believe she wouldn't tell me. This whole time, I thought everything was fine."

Sergei shrugged, as if he could care less about this deeply impactful news. "What about that swim?"

She looked up at his cold face, searching for something she could empathize with. Though his irises were jet black, she noticed he had flecks of gold in them. They were hard to notice at first, and were really only visible in the afternoon light. She noticed that his hair also had subtle brown streaks in it, providing a slight contrast to the blackness. He reminded her of Daman in many ways, with an almost animal-like quality to his features.

"Fine," she said, snapping back to the present. "Let's go swimming."

The pool was shaped like a raindrop and its tiles were hand painted with tangles of green leaves, which Kat had always found odd as it gave off the appearance of algae. Her mother thought it made the pool look dirty, but Kat thought it brought particular warmth, and reminded her of the depths of the ocean. She liked it more than the cold, sterile blue pools typically found in palaces. The patterning of the leaves reminded her of whales— great beasts covered in algae and other types of plankton. Swimming in the pool, pretending to be a mermaid in the deep ocean, had always made her happy.

Outside, the sun was hanging high in the sky. Its rays beat down upon their backs, causing them to drip with sweat.

They walked to opposite sides of the pool, Kat at the shallow end and Sergei at the deep end.

"On the count of three?" she asked.

"One…two!" he shouted, jumping in cannonball style and creating a huge splash. What a clown. Despite herself Kat couldn't help but laugh, and dove under, her body cleaving through the water in a clean arc.

Kat wore a white one-piece bathing suit with a deep v neckline that showed off her ample cleavage. It made her feel more confident to flaunt her body when it could be hidden under water. The white bathing suit also gave hints to her femininity, as her rose tinted nipples got hard in the cold water and pressed tightly against the fabric, as if begging to be freed.

Sergei wore a pair of swim trunks that didn't leave much to the imagination. Kat was tempted for a closer look, and kept stealing glimpses when she knew she wouldn't get caught. His manhood filled out the bathing suit significantly, making her wonder if his excitement was the result of her hard nipples. He looked huge, as if the cold hadn't had any sort of effect on his member.

Suddenly, she remembered something he had said yesterday that had caused her pause.

"Hey, Sergei," she called out to him. "Why did you say it wasn't safe for me to be in the storage room?"

He smirked and dove under the water, swimming long, slow strokes until his hands met her thighs. He emerged from the water and brought his face close to hers.

Was he going to kiss her? She held her breath and realized that she wanted him to.

Instead, he leaned his mouth close to her ear—so close she could feel the warmth of each breath. "I know what he is, because I'm the same." With that, he took her ear in his mouth and sucked long and hard on the lobe, before diving back under water, returning to the other end of the pool.

Confused and unsure if she had heard correctly, she dove underwater to meet him in the deep end. She held tightly onto the edge of the pool, her arms high behind her, as he treaded water next to her.

"Say that again?"

He chuckled, and in one brisk move, took her other ear in his mouth, this time sucking it and holding it between his teeth.

Kat sucked in her breath and felt her skin prickle with excitement.

"That's not what I meant, Sergei."

Sighing, he pulled away, holding her gaze. "I'm the descendant in a long line of Siberian shifters. I'm purebred, which means I haven't been bitten or changed by a shaman. My father and mother were both shifters, as were their parents, and so on. It's obvious you are attracted to shifters, even unawares. And you don't get better stock than me," he answered boldly.

In the bright sunlight, she could notice the flecks of gold dancing around his eyes, and she found it impossible to tear her eyes away from his.

"You're purebred?' she asked. "How fascinating," she teased.

"Only the best for you, princess," he joked, and pressed his body tight against hers. She wrapped her legs around him as she held onto the edge, leaving him no question of her interest. She could feel the warmth of his cock pressing against her delicate mound, and the sensation of being warm all over quickly consumed her.

Kat surprised herself by pressing her body tightly in return, moving ever so subtly against his strained cock. In any other circumstance, she would have swatted him away by now, but she found herself aroused on by his boldness.

Sergei tightened his grip around her waist and traced a finger down Kat's cheek, pausing to slide it gently between her lips. No one had done this to Kat before, but she instinctively closed her lips around his finger and sucked it. He withdrew his finger from her mouth and continued to trace it down her chin and began to trace the outline of each nipple over the thin white fabric. Kat gasped, and he responded by quickly shoving her bathing suit to the side, exposing a perfect breast. She pressed herself into him further, purring at the warmth she felt from traversing from his body into her breast. He continued to journey down her body, pausing at her upper thighs as if to tease her, until finally, his hand slid between her legs. His soft exploring quickly turned to vigorous rhythmic rubbing, and Kat found herself turned on like never before, kissing him roughly, and biting and sucking his full lips. He shoved the fabric of her suit to one side and slid his finger into her wetness. She moaned, biting his lip in response to the arousal, and drawing blood. His cock had forced its way out of the top of his bathing suit and he pressed it against her opening. She had never felt anything like it, and willed her body to push back against his throbbing member, ready to fully submit her body to Sergei.

"Wait, I can't..." she panicked, unwrapping her legs to pull away from Sergei's grip. She scrambled to put her bathing suit back in order and glanced around to see if any of the guards had been watching. The courtyard guard had respectfully turned his back.

"Oh God, that guard has known me since I was three years old. I'm so embarrassed", she said, as she hoisted herself out of the pool and wrapped a towel around her still aroused body.

Sergei emerged somewhat confused from the deep end of the pool and walked towards her, his hard-on still peeking through his shorts.

She pushed him in the chest. "You're terrible," she complained, although what she really wanted to say was, come back here and finish what you started.

"And, you didn't answer my question".

"You heard me the first time—you just want me to say it again. I'm a shapeshifter—a pure blooded one—and I'm not going to let that stray piece of shit that's been lurking around anywhere near that sweet pussy of yours".

Shocked by his brashness, she began to fully absorb what he was saying, and her body started to shiver uncontrollably.

"Are you cold?" he asked.

"I'm...fine..." she said, teeth chattering, and turned to storm away from him. But in one quick moment, the world began to spin.

"Kat! Kat! Someone! Guards!"

7

Kat woke up to the sound of chewing. She glanced to the side of her bed and saw Sergei sitting there. The sun had just gone down and his hair was glowing in the hues of the setting sun. He was eating crackers and staring at her, concerned.

"What are you doing?" she mumbled.

"Waiting for you to wake up so you can eat something," he said gently, offering her a cracker.

"What happened…" she started to ask, but was cut off by a loud knock at the door.

She tried to sit up in bed but Sergei pushed her back down.

"You need rest," he whispered.

She looked up at him, pupils dilated and her heart pumping out of her chest. She was not used to this side of him, and she felt her heart begin to melt. He stared deeply into her eyes, as if he was about to kiss her. But instead of moving in towards her, he pulled away and stood up. When he opened the door, the standing guard informed her that she had a visitor. She could see Daman looming over the shoulder of the guard.

"Well, look at what the cat dragged in," Sergei said quietly.

"Daman, what are you doing here?" Kat asked. She tossed her legs off the bed and walked over shakily.

"It's fine, Alexei" Kat said to the guard.

"I'm sorry to have disturbed you, you're clearly busy," Daman said.

Sergei smirked and draped his hand around Kat's shoulder. "I fainted at the pool," she said. "Or at least I think I fainted. That was the last thing I remember."

"Are you okay?" Daman asked worriedly, reaching out for her hand.

"I'm okay," she said, pulling her hand back. Only hours ago he had rejected her.

Sergei cleared his throat. "How do you two know each other?"

"We met at a party," Daman said gently. He stopped reaching for Kat, but didn't take his eyes off her.

Kat realized she was in the presence of two very different yet equally sexy men. One was seductive and devious; he was, for all intents and purposes, an evil temptation. The other was kind and strong, but respectful, as if holding back from his true desires.

"Why did you come back?"

"I saw your parents driving through town. I was out for a run and thought that maybe you had the house to yourself. I wanted to come by and apologize for my behavior earlier."

"Sergei, could you give us a minute?"

"Sure thing, sweetheart," he said, winking. As he passed by her to leave the room, he dragged his hand slowly across her ass, looking sternly at Daman as if to lay claim to his woman.

Once the door clicked shut, Kat turned to Daman, a pained look on her face.

"Why did you leave so suddenly? I thought you were gone for good. I thought that you never wanted to see me again."

"It's not that at all..." he stammered, but Kat interrupted.

"It's okay. It's fine, really. I understand that you have places to be and people to see. I appreciate you coming back to apologize."

"Could we go for a walk alone, just you and I? I'm sure you have a million questions for me and I want you to be able to ask them. I'll do my best to answer honestly," he said.

"I suppose I could do that," she replied reluctantly, reminding herself that he could run hot and cold.

As they opened the door, Sergei practically fell into the room. He had been leaning against the large oak door.

"Actually, maybe we should all go for a walk together. It seems as though there are things that you each need to say about each other."

The two men stared hard at her in disbelief, before looking sideways at each other before giving reluctant nods of agreement.

Kat smiled and led them out of the house.

They walked across the courtyard, through the cedar hedges, and past the cabbage patch, before following the dark path that led to the edge of the grounds and the forest. The palace was tucked between thick patches of evergreen stands, built hundreds of years ago when land was still plentiful and trees were everywhere. Kat felt bad about the number of trees that had been cleared for their estate, and she knew the minute she gained access to the keep she would start replanting.

When she fantasized about things like this, she imagined the house being surrounded by enormous trees, an endless canopy of green, growing in tangles around her. The pathways would be lined with trees, standing tall and welcoming.

She imagined Sergei pinning her sharply against one of the trees and biting her clavicle. Daman would be there too, on his knees with his face pressed into her wet womanhood. The daydream was so intense and laced with pleasure that she found herself getting warm and blushing at the spot of wetness growing inside her panties.

Kat couldn't understand what was happening to her. When she'd been in the tea room earlier with Sergei, all she could think about was Daman hiding in the closet. But later, when she was in the pool with Sergei, Daman was pushed far from her thoughts. How could she feel such desire for two different men?

When they reached the edge of the path where stone turned to pine needles, they stopped. Daman turned to face Sergei. The moment had come to finally address what was going on between them.

"Have you ever been to this part of the forest before?" he asked.

Sergei looked from Daman to Kat before swallowing once, hard.

"Every once in awhile," Sergei responded with hostility. It was clear he had an issue with Daman.

"Shall we?" Daman asked Sergei. Before he could answer, Daman turned his back, dropped his clothes to the ground and transformed right in front of them. Kat's eyes grew large as she carefully looked him over. His coat was thick and soft and his eyes looked even brighter than before. He was beautiful, and majestic. Kat reached and stroked his head, which he pushed eagerly into her palm. Sergei followed suit, though his was a coat rich with black and blue fur. Of course Sergei was the darker one, Kat thought. He was coy and cunning, and nothing like Daman, who seemed both honest and open.

Kat followed them into the woods, her hands on their backs, each one taking turns to nudge her in the right direction. The pair led her to a clearing with a little river, which fed out into an enormous waterfall. Sergei and Daman dove in, prowling the pool for fish. Kat hesitated for a few seconds. She'd already gone swimming earlier and had fainted. It had been an embarrassing experience, especially because Sergei had been there. But now Daman was here, and for some reason that made her feel safe.

Without giving it another minute's thought, she bravely removed her light green sundress revealing her matching green bra and panties, and jumped into the clear water. It was warmer than she'd expected, and smelled strangely of pine needles and moss.

Sergei and Daman were competing for her affection. They dove through her legs, tickling her, or bit playfully at her ankles. When they finally turned back into humans, they teased her about seeing a princess in so little clothing.

"I could never tell my parents about this," she giggled. "But it sure is nice to do what I want."

"I'm sure Natalia would drop dead if she knew about your extracurricular activities," Sergei said, winking slyly.

Kat splashed water at him. "You're right, though she would probably stop me from ever seeing you again."

Daman watched the exchange between the two with a slightly confused look on his face.

"What are you two talking about?" Daman asked.

Sergei dove under the water for a few seconds as if to stall, before finally resurfacing and spraying the two of them with water.

"If Katerina doesn't find another suitor, the Emerald legacy will crumble," he said, ignoring the question that Daman was really asking.

"I see," said Daman. "But what if Sergei is found unfit?"

"*Me?* You're accusing *me* of being an unfit suitor? Aren't you the one living in squalor off in some dump?" growled Sergei.

Daman's lip twitched slightly, "I live in an apartment, Sergei. I'm sorry I'm not purebred high society like you are."

"Mmm, so you do know who I am," Sergei gloated, a look of boastfulness flashing across his eyes. They continued to stare at each other, saying nothing. Kat watched as their eyes flashed dangerously. Try as she might, she just couldn't walk away, even though deep down she knew that she should. Sergei and Daman were just too attractive, and it was such a turn on that they were fighting over her.

"What happens now?" asked Daman, the first to finally break the silence. "We should probably head back before dark truly sets in."

"Head back where?" The deep voice came from within the forest, and caused all three of them to jump. They turned around, straining their necks, but couldn't see a thing. The trees were thickly woven, and it was difficult to tell if there was somebody out there.

"Who's out there?" Sergei asked, his voice giving away his concern. It was the first time Kat had ever noticed a crack in his armor.

"I have a suspicion," Daman responded. "Just stay cool."

A shadow appeared from behind one of the trees. Whoever he was, he was tall, and wise sounding. Could it be that he was another shifter?

"Dominic, what are you doing here?" Daman asked.

"I heard there was an outsider in my part of the forest. What made you think you could bring a stranger for a swim?

You're not the one in charge around here, Dominic."

Another shifter?! Apparently, she had lead a more sheltered life than she realized.

His voice was deep and gave off an air of authority, though Kat couldn't be sure who he was, or what he wanted with them.

"Why is Miss Emerald here?" he asked, finally acknowledging Kat.

"What of her?" Daman asked. He walked in front of Kat protectively.

Sergei emitted a low growl at Dominic before turning his head to the others and silently motioning to leave.

Together, they walked out of the forest in silence, at a somewhat quickened pace. Kat wasn't sure what had just happened. She couldn't believe there were other tiger shifters apparently all around her. This new one, Dominic, sounded like an older man, and something about him had seemed very familiar.

"Thank you," she said to them when they finally reached the edge of the forest. "That was very heroic of you two for standing your ground."

Confident they had left any threat from Dominic back in the forest, they returned to human form. Kat turned to Daman and kissed him gently on the cheek.

"Hey darlin', don't leave me hanging," Sergei joked. Kat turned to kiss him on the cheek as well, but he turned at the last second and their lips met.

"Oh no," she said, flustered.

"Was it as good for you, as it was for me?" he responded.

"I'll see you guys later," Daman said, rushing away.

"Wait, Daman! When will I see you again?"

But it was too late; he'd already shifted and disappeared back into the woods, jealousy propelling his muscles forward. Sergei shrugged and turned towards the courtyard.

As she walked back to the palace with Sergei, she fell to her knees and clutched her head, as a memory washed over her like an angry wave. It must have been something that she had repressed, for it was a new memory, one of which she had no recollection.

In it Kat was a young girl, with her long hair in two braids. She was wearing a blue dressing gown and brushing her teeth, getting ready for bed. There was a loud commotion in the hallway, and Kat carefully peeked out from the bathroom door. A man had stormed into the palace; a man she had never seen before. He held something silver in his large determined hands. It was an enormous knife, and it reflected the light shining down from the huge crystal chandelier. He had grabbed a hold of her mother and held the huge silver knife to her throat. As Kat watched from the doorway, he threatened to kill her mother. Natalia had seemed paralyzed with fear and wasn't moving or making any noises whatsoever. Kat remembered holding her breath and closing her eyes, expecting the worst. But then a shadow appeared, tackling the intruder, and plunging the knife into his neck.

She was so young when it happened that the tales of the intruder had created and spun memory for her. But after witnessing what she had today, she realized that the shadow had been a Siberian tiger. She was sure of it. The reality of the actual attack now flooded back to her. It *had* been a tiger that had jumped on the intruder, ripping his throat out with his fangs. No wonder her little mind had repressed that memory. She wondered if Dominic, the shifter with the familiar voice had triggered this memory.

Who was that tiger shifter that saved her mother so many years ago ?

Kat could sense Sergei standing over her, concerned. She opened her eyes and stood up slowly, holding out her hand to stop him from speaking.

"I'm fine. It was just a tumble." She knew he didn't believe her, but it was of no concern. Her mind was preoccupied with racing thoughts, struggling to make some order of them.

Someone had mentioned an earlier arrangement—had it been Daman? There was definitely a secret her parents were keeping from her, and she was determined to get to the bottom of it. Perhaps if she dug deep enough, she would find out the true reason her mother was pushing her so hard for marriage to Sergei.

Kat wondered if their status was being challenged. Until Kat fully understood why, she vowed to fight for her family and her legacy. Money be damned; the situation was too important to ignore.

As she and Sergei continued their walk through the safety of the grounds, Kat felt more and more convinced that Daman knew more than he was letting on, and was waiting for the right moment to bring it up. She wanted to ask Sergei to help her draw it out of him. However, once they reached the entranceway, Sergei turned sharply and said goodbye to Kat, before bolting off to his room. She had no chance to ask him if he would participate in her scheme. It would be tough to escape the palace tonight, what with her parents at home and the full guard roster in place. But she would not be deterred.

When darkness fell over the palace, and all the floors had been patrolled, Kat crawled out of bed, not daring to turn on the lights and risk being seen. When she peered out into the hallway, she found it empty.

Sergei's room was just down the hall from her in the library wing. He'd been pompous enough to complain about his guest room, claiming the smell of musty books was keeping him up all night. When Kat reached his door, she didn't bother knocking. Instead, she quietly opened the door, surprised to see him wide-awake reading a dusty paperback.

"I thought you hated old book smell," she mocked.

"Please, come right in without knocking," he responded.

"Why do you always sound like you're mad at me?"

He didn't respond. "I need to ask you a favor," she said, closing the door slowly behind her.

"What's the favor? And don't tell me it involves Daman."

Kat paused. "It involves Daman," she murmured.

Sergei sat up in bed and sighed, debating whether or not he should hear her out. "Continue."

"I want you to come with me to the forest to find him. I need to apologize to him for what happened earlier between you and I."

Sergei sat up straight and slowly put his book down, as a pained look came over his face. He looked into Kat's eyes and whispered quietly, "Was it a mistake?"

"Of course it was," she said quickly. "Just like the pool was a mistake…" her voice trailed off hesitantly.

Sergei took her hesitation as an opportunity and leaned in to kiss her. She heard her breath catch in her throat with surprise. He tugged her forward and onto the bed. She straddled him and they kissed in the stale lamplight. Her body remembered the feel of his kiss and responded before her mind could catch up. She was so turned on that she could feel her wetness soaking through her lace panties. *'Can he feel how wet I am through the sheets?'* she wondered.

He grabbed her around her waist and flipped her over. She was now his prisoner. He pinned her hands to the bed and began to leave a trail of kisses down her neck. He raked his teeth up and down her collarbone, and bit the soft spot beneath her chin. Sergei noticed that she smelled like lavender soap; like she had just come out of the bath. The thought of her naked, her pink nipples peeking through the bubbles, made him rock hard. He lifted up her silky tank top, thrilled at the sight of her taut abs and perky breasts that were covered in goose bumps. He ran his hands up to cup her breasts. She wasn't cold, she was enjoying it. He pressed her breasts together to create a beautiful deep cleavage and rammed his tongue in between them. He bit her right breast and then sucked hard. She gasped at his roughness and arched her back, as if to ask for more. He continued kissing down her stomach while pulling down her silk pajama bottoms, noticing the dampness between her legs. He bit at the top of her panties while his hands continued to massage her breasts. She lifted her hips, signaling to him, and he tugged the lacy fabric down to give him better access to her hot sweetness. He then plunged his face between her legs.

Kat had heard about this, and thought that when a man finally went down on her she would feel awkward, but the moment she felt Sergei's warm breath on her pussy, any trepidation flew out the window. She pushed her hips into his face as he sucked on her lips, and breathed heavily on her clit. Sergei held one hand tightly on her ass and used his free hand to insert one finger into her wetness. She murmured her pleasure and he inserted a second finger, and then a third. She moaned and writhed as he picked up the intensity, thrusting his fingers into her while alternating between teasing her clit with his tongue and sucking madly with his mouth. Her moaning turned to panting, and the panting turned to screaming as she gushed her juices over his face. After she came, the sensitivity of having his face between her legs was too much. She pulled him up to eye level and kissed him as passionately as she could, exalting in her own taste on his lips. She had never felt anything like that. Her body was still tingling and the adrenaline and warmth that had coursed through her was still pulsating and shaking her body.

For the briefest of seconds, all thoughts about Daman had disintegrated. All she could see and feel was Sergei, with his thick hair and eyes the color of the night.

Sergei himself hadn't seen it coming. He could see that there was something between Kat and Daman and that their pool encounter may have been his only shot to impress the Princess. When it was time to turn the lights out he'd found himself tossing and turning for hours. When the clock finally struck twelve, he gave up, turned on the light on and began reading a book. He'd barely gotten past the first page when Kat had entered his room.

He was supposed to be courting Kat, but he could see and feel the strength of the chemistry between her and Daman. And as much as Sergei wanted to hate Daman, he found himself longing for the company of a contemporary. He was the only other male tiger his age he had met, and he wanted to get to know him better. He had contemplated forfeiting his quest to win the Kat in favor of gaining a true pride and friendship with Daman.

I've definitely screwed that up. Daman will probably never forgive me for what happened, but making the her cum like that may have brought her back into my court.

Sergei held Kat close to him as he languidly stroked his rigid cock. Kat was slowly coming out of her orgasmic state and she slid down his body, trailing her hair down his chest as she took his cock in her soft hands. She had never done this before and wasn't quite sure what to do. She licked the sides from the base of his shaft to the tip. It was a little bit salty, but she didn't mind the taste. She kissed the tip of his manhood and took the tip into her mouth. Sergei groaned. She took it as a good sign, and pressed her head down more, attempting to take as much of him as she could into her mouth and throat. Sergei's hips rose and he grabbed a handful of her hair.

"Don't stop."

She pulled her head back and looked up at him while keeping his member in her mouth. His head was back and his mouth was open, producing gruff moans. Feeling her pause, he looked down at her, "Don't you fucking stop."

With her social standing she was never ordered to do anything, and in any other aspect of her life she would've been offended. But his rough tone only made her want to suck him harder. She continued sucking, taking his cock deeply into her mouth before pulling back. She guessed it wasn't quick enough, because Sergei entangled both of his hands in her hair and thrust her head up and down. She continued sucking as he pushed her head, the sucking sounds getting louder and juicier as she salivated over his cock.

"Can you take it?" he uttered.

She didn't know what he meant, and she didn't know how he expected her to answer while her mouth was filled with his pulsating cock. However, it became clear when his hips bucked and he filled her mouth with shot after shot of warm salty cum.

Kat swallowed his load and crawled up his body to kiss him. She thought that two mouths that had just done what they had should be un-kissable, but it was anything but. The smell of her juices on his lips, and the taste of him in her mouth made her want to do it all over again.

He freed his hand from the tangled mess of her hair and patted it down, as if he was petting an animal. She nuzzled into his neck, kissing him gently, and he held her tightly until she heard his breath slow and his hold on her loosen. She looked up at him as he was sleeping and felt more confused than ever. *Was she technically still a virgin?*

She slipped out of his embrace and found her clothes. She crawled up the bed and whispered to him, "I think we should look for Daman now."

"Right now?" he asked, awakening from his peaceful slumber.

He felt a little betrayed and hurt that their passionate encounter had only temporarily made her forget about the other tiger. He had hoped that the physical connection between the two of them would be enough to lure her away from her emotional connection with Daman.

"It's just that I feel bad about how we left things earlier. He's easier to find at night because I know he will be in the forest."

Sergei's interpretation of Kat's intentions was way off. Something had changed in her in that moment of awakening. Kat had started to realize that her position would afford her any privilege , she would be able to do whatever and whomever she wanted. Her orgasm with Sergei had made her hungry for more, and she was now curious to see if Daman would be able to please her the way that Sergei had. This new feeling of power was freeing in a way she'd never experienced before. She was drunk on it.

8

Sergei and Kat entered the forest at half past one, after first making sure that the palace guards were in between patrols. Sergei instructed Kat to remain cautious and to keep her eyes and ears peeled for any potential danger, as he got on his hands and knees and transformed. Though she'd seen him this way just a few hours ago, it still shocked her to see the brilliant blacks and blues of his coat, shining in the moonlight. She scratched the space behind his ears, thrilled by the deep purr that her touch brought out. She had no idea that big cats purred the same as little ones.

"Let's head in the direction of the waterfall first."

He nodded his big cat head and began to lope forward, his huge paws padding silently on the forest floor. The forest was thick and dark green, with pools of moonlight spilling through the gaps in the trees. Even though she was with Sergei, she felt on edge. There were other animals living in the forest that she'd never seen before. She knew it was ridiculous to be scared. After all, there was a tiger walking next to her. Shouldn't she feel completely safe?

Sergei felt his heart pounding in his chest. He was developing intense feelings for Kat but didn't know what to do about any of them. It left him feeling very vulnerable and he didn't like it. The right thing to do would be to propose and lock her down. His father had already given him a ring, an old family heirloom, and it would be easy enough to ask her. But there was also the question of how Daman would play into all of it. How could he maintain a friendship with Daman and at the same time, win the heart of this woman?

In the distance, two poachers greedily watched the pair through night vision binoculars as they walked through the forest. It was a couple—a man and woman that had been poaching in the area for the past two years, specializing in hunting rare animals. Several times, the armed forces had tried to capture them and each time they had failed. The woman went by Raven—a fitting name for such a dark, dangerous personality—and the man's name was Gunner. They were a pair of Americans who were hungry for money, not giving any thought to the conservation of animals or endangered species. To them, a Siberian tiger was a once-in-a-lifetime catch, and a big paying one at that.

Raven had been the first one to spot it. She'd never seen a tiger with such a rich coat of fur. It was black and blue, like a soft bruise, and it would definitely fetch them a huge sum of money. Walking beside the magnificent beast was a pretty young girl, dressed in expensive silk.

Raven elbowed Gunner hard in the ribs. "Do you see that?"

"Mmm," he responded, while trying to keep as quiet and still as possible.

"The only people around here who have the resources to tame a beast like that are the Emerald family. How are we going to shoot the pet of the Emerald heiress?"

"You're thinking too small. She could be valuable, too," Gunner responded, a greedy look in his eyes. He picked up his rifle and carefully followed the duo through his night scope.

"Should we go for them now?" she asked.

"Not yet. Let's see where they're headed."

They didn't have to follow for very long. The tiger and the girl stopped at a magnificent waterfall. The tiger seemed to want to go for a swim, pushing her with its head towards the pool at the base of the waterfall. Raven carefully strained her eyes; she was curious, it seemed to her that the girl and the tiger were communicating. She half expected the tiger to begin speaking, but shook off such foolishness. As tough and cold-hearted as she was, it would make hunting more challenging having to kill something that could speak back to her.

Gunner decided to approach first. He gave Raven his gun and approached the pair slowly, with his hands raised in the air. As he entered the moonlit clearing, they turned at the sound, and immediately froze. The young woman's eyes grew wide, full of fear and confusion. The tiger stepped protectively in front of her, emitting a low growl. He clearly had some kind of companionship with her.

"I don't want any trouble," Raven could hear Gunner saying in his broken Russian. "I just want to have a conversation with you," he said, looking directly at Kat.

"Who are you?" She replied in English, coated with her thick Russian accent. "I've never seen an American around these parts before."

"How could you tell I was American?"

"Your Russian is terrible," she laughed, momentarily letting her guard down.

Gunner shrugged, taking a step closer.

"He'll kill you if you get any closer to me," Kat said.

"Somehow I doubt that," Gunner said, and in one swift movement, he lunged forward and shot a tranquilizer into the tiger's neck.

Sergei could feel the world spinning as he became dizzy. The sky looked like a misshapen egg and all around him there were monsters. He tried to crane his neck to look for Kat, but his muscles were contracting and strangling his bones. The only thing he could manage to do was try to call for help. Struggling, he carefully emitted a loud, painful wail, to try and alert any other animals in the forest of the danger. Even though he was a stranger to this part of the forest, he had the instinct to call for help and he had been well trained by his father for how to signal danger. It was the same call everywhere.

From deep within the forest, Dominic heard Sergei's call of distress and frantically ran in the direction that it came from. Staying hidden in the shadows, he witnessed the male poacher tying ropes tightly around Sergei's paws, while the female poached kept her gun trained on Kat.

He knew that he would have to find backup. Frantically searching his territory, he was dismayed that he couldn't find Daman anywhere. He let out a call to attract others of his kind nearby and they heeded the call. They quickly gathered around him in a circle.

"Where is Daman?"

"Probably off being human," replied one of the smaller tigers. "He's been kicking around that run-down apartment of his for the past few weeks, doing who knows what."

"Take me there."

The other tiger was too afraid of the human world to leave the forest, but managed to get Dominic to the edge of town and then gave him instructions on how to get there. Dominic bolted off into the night. He needed to find Daman before it was too late, and before one of his kind was lost to needless poaching. However, Dominic was more worried about Kat. His stomach turned at the thought of something happening to her.

Kat was draped over Gunner's shoulder, her hands tied behind her back. He had given her a milder tranquilizer meant for small game, which had taken effect almost immediately. He smirked to himself as he traipsed through the forest. Raven had been worried it would be a difficult mission. They hadn't needed to use any of their ammunition, and were still well stocked should the need arise.

They arrived at base camp after an hour's walk, and quickly hooked up the trailer to an ATV. There was no way they would have been able to drag the tiger that far, and besides, the dragging would have ruined his valuable pelt. The camp was near a thin strip of river, camouflaged by large weeping willow trees. They couldn't have found a better hiding spot. Gunner quickly headed off into the forest and returned with Sergei strapped to the trailer.

The pair placed Sergei and Kat in separate cages, suspending them from branches the same way that they suspended their food, so it wouldn't attract any bears.

"What if they fall?" Raven asked.

"Well, it will make our job with the tiger a lot easier, but it will be harder to get payment for a dead girl," Gunner replied, adding a second knot to the ropes that held the cages.

They had no sense of right or wrong; poaching was the only thing they knew how to do.

When Kat awoke, her arms and back were stiff. She grimaced as she turned to her right, barely able to make out a dark form hanging in a metal cage next to her. Shaking, she dared to look at the ground, and instantly became sick. She was locked in a cage high up off the ground—about twenty feet or so—and she wondered how the American had managed to do it on his own. He'd clearly had help.

This is all my fault, she thought to herself. *If I hadn't fallen for the two of them, we wouldn't be in this situation. Perhaps I should have listened to mother and just married Sergei.*

As Kat thought more about her involvement in their dire situation, she reasoned with herself. *Although, had it not been for Sergei and I getting caught, the poachers may have caught Daman or others like him. The forest isn't safe until they rid it of these monsters.*

As she lay curled in the small metal cage, mourning her fate, Kat longed for Daman—both for the help he could give, and for his comforting embrace,

Below, she could see Gunner starting a fire. Kat thought it was quite foolish of him to be starting a fire in the middle of the forest, but then she noticed the small arsenal of weapons by his side. There were all sorts of guns she'd never seen before. These people had come prepared.

She needed to find a way to escape. And after that, she needed to figure out a way to keep both Daman and Sergei by her side.

Kat struggled to untie her wrists. The man had tied the knots tightly, and she was having trouble escaping the thick rope. It was digging into her wrists, and the more she struggled, the tighter the rope seemed to get.

She was so distracted working on the rope, that at first she didn't notice the two dark figures approaching the camp site. What she did notice, however, were the pile of bones haphazardly tossed into the brush beside the campsite. Kat shuddered thinking about how many animals had lost their lives at the hands of poachers? They were selfish beings, wanting animal pelts and teeth for their own enjoyment. Sometimes she hated being human.

Down below, Daman and Dominic had entered the camp. It had been ages since they had hunted together, and it felt good to be working in a team again. Daman had forgotten what it meant to be part of a tiger shifter streak, becoming wrapped up in depression over losing his family members, and more recently, his growing interest in Kat. But Dominic was here now, by his side, putting his life on the line for him.

Daman had been hanging out on the seventh floor of an abandoned apartment, and was soaking in an old, claw-toothed bathtub when he felt a tiger's presence; it took him a few moments to realize it was Dominic. Though naked, Daman had stood up and embraced his old friend.

"What are you doing here?" he asked.

"You know I wouldn't be here if it wasn't important. There's trouble in the forest," Dominic had said, after returning to his human f0rm. "Sergei and Kat have been captured by poachers."

Daman's face turned white, and he struggled to speak. He shook his head as if he hadn't heard right.

"Poachers, Daman." Dominic repeated.

The word rocked Daman to his core, and the feelings that overcame him were so intense that he thought he might pass out. It was poachers who had set the fire that had killed his mother and brother, and now once again, it was poachers who had taken the one person he cared for.

Daman couldn't bear the thought of anything happening to Kat; nor Sergei, who he could see himself one day befriending. The only way he could see this ending well for any of them, would be to kill the poachers.

"Good thing I'm starving. I don't usually find humans tasty, but tonight I think I could go for a little roasted poacher," he winked.

Daman smiled a toothy grin, biting back the fear that sat deep within his throat. "I think I just got my appetite back."

They'd bounded into the forest together as tigers, their hearts beating out of their chests for different reasons. Dominic was afraid for Kat's life, whereas Daman feared seeing Kat again. He hadn't been able to get her out of his mind for weeks now. She was every bit as elegant and beautiful as he had thought she'd be, but even more so when he was up close to her. The accidental kiss that he had witnessed between Sergei and Kat didn't bother him; he could get over that. What did bother him was thinking about Kat in danger, which caused him to extend his stride and sprint even faster.

Dominic purred to Daman, signaling that they needed to be silent as they approached. Their breathing became shallow and they hunched back on their hind legs, preparing to pounce. Gunner and Raven had their backs turned to the forest, and they appeared to be cleaning their guns. They were unprepared for an ambush from behind.

When Dominic gave the signal, a low throaty cry, Daman rushed forward and pounced on Gunner. It had sounded eerie, almost childlike, and was meant to scare prey.

Dominic pounced on Raven, biting her on the back of her neck, hard. Their attack was messy, and left a sticky blood trail around the circumference of the fire. It was over for the poachers before they'd known what happened. The bloodlust overtook the two shifters and they did as a true tiger would. They feasted. When they were finished eating their prey and were satisfied, Daman transformed back to human form. He stood up and scratched the bigger, older cat behind his ears, before Dominic disappeared back into the forest. Daman buried the weapons so they could never again be used to harm a forest dweller, but he left the stained bloody clothes as a warning to other poachers.

Next, he turned his attention to the cages. Kat was watching from above, still drowsy from the tranquilizer. She had turned away when they'd first attacked, not wanting to witness the brutal violence, although she realized it had been necessary. She clung to the sides of the cage as Daman lowered her to the ground, careful not to crush her legs dangling through the bars. He grabbed an axe and struck the cage once, the lock snapping off. Kat crawled out of the cage and stretched her stiff legs, before leaping into Daman's arms, kissing him hard on the cheek. She wanted to kiss him deeply, but after witnessing what he had just snacked upon, decided against it.

"Thank you," she murmured.

"You're, uh, welcome," he replied, struggling to find words.

When Sergei was released he could barely stand without assistance. His legs were like flimsy noodles and his body felt like it weighed a thousand pounds.

"What happened?" he managed to croak, not yet able to use his full voice.

"You were captured by poachers," Daman told him. He stuck a thumb into his chest and said, "But Dominic and I saved you."

Sergei eyes shone with gratitude; his human body covered in dust and dirt. He still had tufts of tiger fur in his hair. Remnants of his other self often remained when he was forced to transform. Whenever he felt too sick to maintain his tiger form, his body forced the transformation back into a human. Fortunately the poachers hadn't noticed the change. Seeing Kat there, he was thankful that this time it had just been his hair. Once, he'd transformed back, only to find a long tail growing out of his back. It had taken him many years to learn how to transform flawlessly between tiger and human, but even now, there were times that his body fought the change. He blamed it on being purebred. The tiger was especially strong in him.

"Nice hair," Kat said weakly.

Sergei smiled and nodded, before giving in and closing his eyes. They were heavy with exhaustion, and he found he couldn't keep them open anymore.

"Get her back to the palace," Sergei ordered Daman. "I should be well enough to get back to the palace by morning."

Daman nodded and held out his hand to Kat. He helped her to her feet, but seeing how wobbly she was, picked her up in his arms in one smooth motion. He carried her gently, walking slowly to the keep and cutting through the garden to avoid the guards.

"I'm going to put you down for a moment," he told Kat once they were safely hidden next to the garden wall, nestled amongst pumpkins. The orange of them reminded Kat of Daman's soft tiger fur.

"Mmm," she responded. She was sleepy, and didn't want to get up to walk inside quite yet. The night was beautiful, and she could see the North star from their resting spot on the ground.

Daman lay next to her, staring up at the stars, and took her hand in his. They stayed like that for a few minutes before Daman's instincts got the best of him, and he turned to kiss her. It surprised her, and the adrenaline that shot through her body made her eyes crisp and alert. She was overcome by both lust and gratitude, as Daman had been the one to save her from certain doom. He pushed her back onto the grass and planted soft kisses up her wrists and shoulders. The way Daman touched her was softer, and more docile than Sergei. Sergei had been hungrier, acting like he would explode if he didn't touch her with ferocity.

Daman's breath was warm, causing her skin to erupt into goosebumps. He touched her lightly all over, and she found herself becoming wet as a result of his touch. He reached beneath the folds of her clothing and began to massage her breasts while kissing her deeply. She felt an incredible warmth rush through her body which soothed her. They continued to kiss passionately, unaware that back in the palace Natalia had risen from her sleep to check on Kat.

Yet again, thoughts of her daughter had turned to worry, for no reason she could put her finger on, other than a mother's instinct. She had loved watching her daughter sleep since a young age, and felt drawn to do so tonight. However, even with the faint moonlight shining through the window, she could see that the bed was empty. Kat was gone.

Enraged by her daughter's disappearance, she flew out the front door into the courtyard. She knew there was a chance Kat would be there, as she had often found her daughter out playing with the fireflies, or doing midnight gardening, when she should be tucked into her bed. For an only daughter, she could be quite a handful. But she didn't find Kat there, either. Natalia screamed out Kat's name, worried.

Kat heard her mother's screams from the garden. She reluctantly tore herself from Daman's embrace, and quickly tugging the fabric of her dress over her bare shoulders.

"You must go," she hissed to Daman. He nodded, and did a semi-bow. Kat giggled and then turned to the palace and hurried inside, ready to face her mother's wrath.

9

The next morning, Natalia was in a foul mood and ignored her daughter as she sat across the breakfast table. She was still angry with Kat for sneaking out in the dark, even though it didn't technically constitute running away. When Kat had returned inside to face her mother, she'd been covered in dirt and smelled like the earth. Natalia had demanded she take a bath, and even though it was very late and all the maids were sleeping, Kat had begrudgingly complied.

She was exhausted from dealing with the poachers, though a larger part of her was still heated from being with Daman. They'd been interrupted, but at least they had gotten to be alone in each other's company for more than a few minutes.

"Why in Heaven's name would you go out in the middle of the night? Why can you not wait until morning like everyone else? What are you smirking at? Do you think it's funny you were out all night in the garden? I thought you had been kidnapped. What would have happened to you then? Who would come and save you?"

"I'm fine," Kat spat back. She didn't like it when her mother treated her like a child; she was perfectly capable of saving herself. Well, she was perfectly capable of being rescued by the two shifters in her life. Now that she had patched things up with Daman, she knew she could count on having him by her side. She wondered if he had gotten home okay.

Natalia eyed Kat across the breakfast table. Her free-spirited daughter was going to send her to an early grave. If Kat didn't marry soon and hopefully produce and heir, their empire would go to the next best option—Kat's cousin, Olysia. Kat and her cousin had never really bonded, even as young girls. Olysia would be traveling to the palace for a few weeks on business. Natalia pondered how to break this news to her daughter.

When Natalia had finished her breakfast and left the dining hall, Kat glared at Sergei. "How did you even get home last night? I thought you were still passed out!"

"Shh," he said. "Your mother's probably eavesdropping in the room next to us, and I don't want her worrying about me. Besides, I got back fine. The tranquilizers wore off after an hour, and so I simply walked back to the palace."

"How did you get past the guards at such a late hour?"

"The guards know me. And we have a working relationship."

Kat rolled her eyes. "Of course you do. How much did that cost you."

"So, I see that Daman got you back here in one piece…" he trailed off.

Kat felt herself blush, but didn't respond.

So what's this I hear about your cousin coming to town?"

"What? This is the first I'm hearing of this" Kat said, clearly annoyed.

She'd always been jealous of Olysia and her natural beauty. She was taller than Kat, almost six feet, and had bronzed skin subtly covered with freckles. Her eyes were the same mixture of green and blue as Kat's and she had the same long hair, but something about Olysia always made Kat feel short and inadequate. Kat was thin, whereas Olysia was tall and curvy, and she liked to show off her huge breasts and round ass in revealing dresses— dresses that Kat found a little on the skanky side.

"You don't like your cousin?" Sergei prodded. Though he was now closer with Kat than ever before, he still received great pleasure from finding what annoyed her, and then pushing those buttons.

"She's fine," Kat said tersely, pushing food around her plate. "Do you want to go for a walk before she gets here?"

"Okay," he said slowly. "But are you sure you want to go back into the forest? The last time you suggested it, you got us kidnapped."

"I know, and I'm sorry. But this time will be different. Besides, it's daylight. What could go wrong?"

Sergei agreed reluctantly, mostly so he could have alone time with Kat, away from her mother's prying eyes. Kat wandered upstairs to tell her mother she was leaving with Sergei, but Natalia was on her phone. She abruptly halted her conversation, held up one slender diamond covered finger, and dismissed her from the room. Obviously she didn't want Kat to hear the conversation. Kat was only too happy to oblige. As she skipped down the hallway, excited to have some freedom with Sergei, she stopped in her tracks. There on the front stairway was her cousin, talking with Sergei, one hand on his shoulder, the other on his hip.

"Oh, hey there," said Olysia, in a voice so low and sultry, Kat couldn't be sure who exactly it was intended for.

"Hi Olysia."

As much as she was bothered by Olysia, she tried to be cordial. "When did you get here?"

"Just now. My father's been held up with meetings again, and isn't sure if he'll make it. I'm sure your mother's on the phone with him right now. It looks like I'll be staying with your family for the next few weeks."

Kat wasn't sure how to react to this news, but before she could respond, Olysia draped her arm around Sergei's shoulders. "So, where are we headed?"

"We were just about to go for a walk in the forest."

"Sounds wonderful, I'd love to stretch my legs. I've been in the car for hours."

"I don't think that those heels are going to cut it" Kat said, motioning to Olysia's red stilettos.

"Oh, don't you worry. I've gotten into hiking." Olysia turned and yelled to one of the doormen, "fetch me my footwear suitcase".

Olysia stamped her feet into her hiking boots, the rugged boots looking truly ridiculous matched up with her designer sheath dress. "Let's do this!"

Kat couldn't help herself, she smirked at the thought of Olysia's reaction to seeing a tiger shifter. She was a city girl, and even with her expensive hiking boots, she was not going to deal well with the wildlife they were about to experience.

Kat also had a terrible feeling in the pit of her stomach. She wasn't thrilled at the body language she had just walked in on, and hoped that finding out about Sergei's secret would scare Olysia far, far, away.

Though she'd hated the outdoors when they were younger, Olysia seemed to flourish in the warm weather and bright green grass. As they walked across the courtyard, the wind had picked up and was blowing against their faces and whipping their hair.

As soon as they crossed the threshold to the forest, darkness enveloped them. It was sticky and warm, and a nice change from the cold, brisk morning at the palace. They found Daman in his tiger form, lazing beneath a large oak tree, dozing in the heat. Kat cleared her throat and Daman turned to face her. Kat could feel Olysia move behind her, cowering in fear.

"Do you think it will attack us?" Olysia whispered, shaking.

"No. He's a friend of mine. Daman, I'd like you to meet my cousin."

At the mentioning of his name, Daman quickly transformed into his human form. He swept low to the ground and carefully picked up his stack of clothes, holding them in front of his manhood for modesty's sake, and bowing to Olysia.

"Delighted to make your acquaintance," he grinned.

To give Olysia credit, she certainly could roll with a surprise. She giggled nervously and held out a hand to him. "Were you cursed by a shaman?"

"I don't think so," Daman replied. "I can shift into my tiger form without the assistance of a full moon, which is generally the stuff of fairy tales."

"And what about you handsome?" Olysia asked, pointing at Sergei. "Are you a tiger as well?"

"Hold onto your hat m'lady" Sergei growled in a low voice, not wanting to be upstaged. He quickly ripped off his shirt and dropped his pants, causing Olysia to gasp. He then leapt into the air, his body changing as if it were jumping through an invisible hula-hoop.

"Wow, look at the color of his fur," purred Olysia, grinning slyly. She let her hands glide slowly over Sergei's back, which elicited a loud purr, much to the dismay of Kat. He rolled over onto his back, allowing Olysia to stroke his belly. Though she had been afraid a few seconds ago, she certainly didn't look scared at all. Kat found it a little odd that she wasn't more nervous about what was happening right in front of them. Why, she hadn't seemed even the least bit hesitant to pet Sergei. Kat began to feel slightly territorial.

"So, what brings you all to the forest?" Daman asked. "Not that I'm unhappy to see you."

"My mother is throwing a masquerade ball tomorrow evening. Would you like to come? Kat had swiped an invite from the maid's room and handed it to him. It was black and embossed in gold calligraphy. It's the perfect place to be anonymous." Kat said and thought back to the magical night that their eyes had first met.

"Natalia is throwing a ball? I had no idea! I'm so excited! Where can I get a costume?" Olysia squealed.

Kat turned to Olysia, annoyed that she had ruined her moment with Daman. "It's a masquerade ball, so wear something flashy. But don't forget to wear a mask. I think the guards will be handing them out at the door."

Daman felt honoured and proud she had asked him, especially in front of Sergei. Sergei had rolled the dice on whether to use Olysia's obvious interest to make Kat jealous. But fortunately for Daman, Sergei's jealousy plan had backfired.

"I would love to attend the ball, but my tuxedo is at the cleaners." Daman replied.

"I'll take care of that." Olysia said. "Give me your address and I'll have a suit sent over. It would be a damn shame for a fine man like you to miss one of Natalia's parties."

"I can't accept that." Daman responded, looking down to the ground.

"Nonsense. If you do not come to the ball and dance with me, I will make your life miserable." Olysia said, reaching up and taking Daman's chin in her hand. "You don't want to be on my bad side."

Kat felt her face flush red in anger.

Sergei sat on the sidelines smirking at the obvious power struggle emerging between the two women. *This could get interesting*, he thought to himself.

"Then it's settled." Olysia said firmly. "Let's all plan to meet up by the indoor pool around eight tomorrow night then, shall we?"

"Sure" Kat murmured, not wanting to seem difficult.

10

The night of the party, the palace was bustling with sequined and masked partygoers. There were three guards at the door handing out masks to anyone who didn't have one.

Daman had seemed annoyed by Olysia's gesture, or threat, but there wasn't much he could do, considering his circumstances. He would do anything to spend more time close to Princess Kat.

However, doubt had begun to creep in. Perhaps he should turn his attentions to someone else. He had intense feelings for Kat, but being with her was complicated with Sergei in the picture. Sergei had so much more to offer her, and Natalia was pushing for their marriage. The more he thought about it, the more he realized it might be easier to bed Olysia.

He technically wasn't a suitable mate for courting Olysia either, but he could definitely seduce her. He could smell the lust in her.

Olysia and Sergei arrived first. Kat was preoccupied in the ballroom talking to what her mother referred to as, 'important people'. Finally, when she was able to slip away, she whisked off towards the indoor pool, excited to see both Daman and Sergei. Kat was pleased with her evening look—a long turquoise gown with a low-cut back. The front was demure and suitable for a future queen, but the back portrayed a more playful side. She was also wearing a bright blue mask with peacock feathers fanning out around her face. She had never felt more beautiful, and her stomach was full of butterflies of anticipation for how the night would unfold.

She burst into the humidity of the pool room to see Olysia and Sergei standing with their bodies pressed tightly against each other. Sergei was stroking Olysia's long blonde hair. She cleared her throat loudly.

"What the hell?" she yelled. "Sergei?"

"Is there a problem, Princess?"

Kat was lost for words and she turned and ran out the room. As she made a left, she ran straight smack dab into Daman's chest.

"Where are you running off to?" he asked. "I just got here."

"Sergei and—and Olysia...." she couldn't finish her sentence before tears starting running down her cheeks.

"Why does it bother you?" he asked, confused. "I thought you wanted me here tonight? You have me so confused."

"I don't know! I'm sorry! I have these intense feelings and I don't know what to do with them. One minute I have feelings for you, and the next I'm lusting after Sergei. Is it even possible to be in love with two people at the same time?"

"I don't know," Daman said kindly. "But I'm sure your heart will help you figure it out. In the meantime, let's go for a walk so you can clear your head. I've always wanted to check out that enormous telescope everyone in the town is always talking about."

She nodded and followed him silently down the hall, biting back what was left of her tears. Daman was right; she needed to count on her heart to sort things out. But what was she supposed to do when her heart wanted both of them at the same time? They were like her two dark princes, always there for her when she needed them. And now, one had been taken from her.

When they reached the astronomy room, Daman froze in astonishment. Inside, was an enormous glass dome showcasing the night sky. The room, though dark, seemed brightly lit from the thousands of bright stars shining through it—an almost other-worldly glow.

"I can't believe this place is real," Daman murmured. "Although I don't know why I'm surprised. You do live in what is essentially a castle, after all."

"Estate, or palace, if you will." she corrected him.

"Kat, I have to ask you, something important," Daman said suddenly, turning towards her and taking her hands into his own.

"What is it?" she asked, bracing herself for the worst.

"Will you dance with me? We never got to dance together that night that we first met."

She laughed, bowing her head towards him. Now that they were away from the echoing hallways and cluster of people, they could hear the soft jazz spilling into the room. Combined with the starlight, it was the most romantic place for a first dance. She allowed herself to forget everything that was happening in the world around her—including Sergei and Olysia—and leaned her head on Daman's chest for comfort as they swayed to the melodic beat.

11

"What is going on here?" screamed Natalia. Kat nearly jumped out of her skin. They had been so caught up in the music and romance of the moment that neither had noticed her enter the room.

"Mother, it's just a dance," Kat tried to explain.

"*Just* a dance? But where is Sergei? And who is this man? I've never seen him before."

Kat was at a loss for words and couldn't think up an appropriate story for Daman, especially on the spot.

"Come to think of it, he looks strangely familiar," Natalia muttered, as she carefully scrutinized the stranger that continued to hold her daughter in a close embrace.

Kat shrugged her shoulders. "Mother, could you give us a moment, please? Sergei is off somewhere with Olysia, and Daman has been a comfort to me."

"No. You will march out of this room and find Sergei, and ask him to forgive you for whatever it is that happened. And then you two *will* start planning your wedding. Come now." She reached out her thin, bony hand and grabbed her daughter's arm.

"NO!" screamed Kat, feeling brave for the first time in her life. But Natalia wouldn't listen, and she dragged her out of the room by her arm, leaving Daman alone, unable to help.

When Natalia was like this, she was inconsolable, and Kat knew that there was nothing she could say or do to make the situation any better. But the memory of Daman's face as she was dragged away would be forever cemented in her mind. As they had danced in the moonlight, she had dared herself to dream about a future with Daman. Maybe Sergei wasn't the best choice, and with the way she had been feeling lately—brave and adventurous for the first time in her life—was all because of Daman. She wanted to tell Daman she would abandon the inheritance for him, and had been working up the courage to ask him to run away with her, when they were interrupted by Natalia. Of course, it was fast and they hadn't slept together yet, but the passion was there. And it gave Kat something to look forward to.

"What in Heaven's name are you thinking about now?" her mother asked.

"What are you talking about?" Kat asked. "You're dragging me by my arm like a child; what do you *think* I'm thinking right now?"

"Oh, Katerina, why can't you see that you are making a terrible mistake?"

She didn't know how to respond to her mother. It seemed better to remain silent, and to allow her to be dragged along like a rag doll.

When they reached the pool, they found Sergei and Olysia perched on two teak lounge chairs, sipping martinis. Olysia had her toothpick in her mouth and was seductively sucking on the olive. When Olysia saw Kat, she grinned a sly grin that was more tigress than sheep.

"You," Natalia said, pointing at Olysia. "GO. And you two, stay. I think there is a conversation that needs to take place," she said, nudging Kat towards Sergei.

Olysia got up to leave, but as she did she leaned down and placed a lingering kiss on Sergei's cheek. He whispered something to her and she nodded, before sauntering out of the room. Olysia was both beautiful and malicious.

"Hi," Kat mumbled to Sergei. He smiled at her.

"Hi, back."

Natalia left the room, leaving them completely alone.

"I don't understand what happened," Kat said, honestly. "I thought that everything was going well between us."

"Well now, sweetheart, we aren't exactly in a committed relationship, are we? I mean, who do you want—me or Daman? You keep teasing and toying with the two of us, so why shouldn't I be allowed to do the same, and hook up with whomever I want?"

Surprised by his candor, Kat struggled to find the right words.

Because I'm selfish and I want both you and Daman at the same time? What is my problem? Say something, Kat. Don't just sit there in silence.

But when she opened her mouth to speak, no words came out. She realized Sergei was right. It wasn't fair for her to string along two men who both cared equally for her. She would have to pick one of them. It was impossible for a Queen to have two Kings.

"My mother asked for me to forgive you," Kat said, quietly.

"Forgive *me*? Whatever for?"

"You must know how much it hurt me to see you with Olysia earlier, and even just now. You can't deny that."

"I don't."

"Then what happens next?"

They stared at each other, an unspoken desire filling the room, until Sergei finally broke the silence. "Do you want to go for a swim?" he asked.

"No. I should go find Daman and apologize."

"That's all you do!" Sergei yelled, losing his cool. "Constantly apologizing to him for running away again and again? When are you going to realize that you two just aren't right for each other?"

"Like *you're* right for me?"

"Well. I'm rich."

"I can't believe you," she cried. "When we first met, I thought your obtuse attitude was just an act to push me away. But I'm beginning to realize more and more that it isn't an act; you're actually a superficial person, Sergei. And I don't want to be with you, let alone forgive you or marry you."

"Kat, wait—" he pleaded. But it was too late; she'd already left the room. It wasn't worth her time to hear Sergei beg for her to stay.

Kat stomped down the hall on a mission to find Daman. If there were a chance he was still there, then she would find him.

Women in sparkling dresses flitted up and down the hallways and there were small children darting in and out of the crowd, wearing whiskers and cat ears.

She rushed back to the astronomy room but her heart sank when she saw that it was empty. She sighed and began to sulk away, when she heard faint purring—no, snoring—coming from a dark corner. Venturing into the darkness, she found Daman curled up in an enormous armchair, a book spread out open on his lap. On closer inspection, Kat noticed it was a full-color version of *The Divine Comedy*. She'd always loved Dante's Inferno, even though it had shocked and disturbed her.

There was a part she especially loved, when Dante meets up with Beatrice. In real life, she had been his true love, but she had died at a young age. He wrote about her in his work of fiction, and she was turned into an angel of sorts. Kat always thought she sounded like the most beautiful woman in the entire world. Dante could barely even look at her without squinting, for she was brighter and on a higher plane than he was.

Why had no one ever looked at Kat that way? The closest she'd come was the way Sergei had looked at her while pinning her to the bed. Like a butterfly with her wings on display, all her emotions and thoughts had spread out from her face and into her arms and legs. Daman still hadn't dared to look at Kat that way, at least not to her face. He had only watched her from afar, as she was a beautiful and curious thing to him, a treasure of sorts—yet another way that he was different from Sergei.

As if he could read her thoughts, Daman slowly opened his eyes, smiling as he noticed Kat's presence.

"I can't believe you're still here," she whispered.

"Where's Sergei?" he asked, still smiling.

"He's off with Olysia doing God knows what. I spoke to both him and my mother. She really wants me to forgive him. He thinks that because we aren't exclusively dating, that he should be allowed to do whatever he wants."

"Are *we* dating?" Daman asked.

"You and I?"

"Well, I guess all three of us," he laughed.

She sighed and sat down gently on his lap, leaning her head back against his neck. "I honestly have no idea anymore."

He chuckled and began to run his fingers up and down her collarbone. She sighed and leaned back against him, grinding her hips into his.

From across the room, she could hear the large heavy door creak open. Daman pressed his strong hand over her mouth. For some reason, Kat found this to be a huge turn on, and she pressed her ass harder into his lap, feeling his erection press against her womanhood. If she couldn't have both of them, she was happy to have this moment with Daman. She could hear silent padding around the room, and was tempted to peak over the armchair to see who it was, but that would blow their perfect hiding place.

Kat knew of a secret doorway built into one of the nearby bookshelves. It led to a small library—a perfect spot for her and Daman to explore each other's bodies for the first time. If the ghost in the room would only leave, she and Daman could run off together.

Kat's breath caught as the footsteps did just the opposite, turning in the direction of the armchair. Her heart climbed into her throat as the steps came closer and closer, making it hard to breathe. She was so worried they were going to be caught by another guest, someone who would know for certain that Daman didn't belong there. Finally, a hand appeared around the edge of the armchair, followed by a body. It was Sergei, and he looked distraught.

"What are you doing here?" asked Kat, surprised.

"I thought I should come and apologize to you. I don't know what came over me back there—I definitely wasn't thinking straight. To be honest, you make me nervous, princess. I'm not used to having such strong feelings about anyone."

Daman and Kat didn't say anything, though they knew exactly how Sergei felt. It was a complicated love triangle, and they were all having trouble keeping track of their emotions. Kat could hear Olysia calling out for Sergei from down the hall. Sergei leaned further into the armchair, pressing into Kat and Daman, attempting to hide. Daman protectively put his arm around Sergei and pulled him in close, sheltering him from the glow of the room.

"Sergei?" called Olysia, her high heels echoing on the hardwood floor. It sounded like she was close. "Where did you go?"

Sergei didn't respond, but Kat could feel his hot breath on her ear. As she leaned her head back against Daman, she could see Sergei's lustful stare from the corner of her eye. With a smirk, he leaned in and licked her neck. After a few minutes, Olysia seemed to give up, and disappeared back down the hallway.

"That was a close one," Daman said.

"Agreed," Sergei responded.

"I have an idea," Kat said, feeling emboldened after almost being caught by Olysia. Somehow, she managed to tear herself away from the comfort of the armchair, and walked over to the bookshelf, frantically pressing and pulling on anything that might open the passageway. After what felt like countless failed attempts, she tugged on an old hardcover that was decorated in Latin. The bookshelf slowly swung away from them to reveal a cobblestone pathway into darkness.

"What is this?" Sergei breathed.

"When I was younger it used to be a library with controversial books from the revolution. I guess we'll have to go exploring to see for ourselves." And with that she grabbed both of their hands and pulled them into the darkness.

Sergei and Daman looked at each other and shrugged.

The tunnel fed out into an enormous library, and it was just as Kat remembered from her childhood. There weren't any doors or windows, only enormous golden chandeliers from the turn of the century. The room was full of plush red velvet couches, smooth wooden tables, and a huge fireplace.

Daman set to work lighting a fire to take away some of the dampness from the room, while Sergei plopped down lazily on one of the couches.

"So, what do we do now?" Sergei asked greedily, pulling Kat towards him.

"I was thinking we should finish what we started," Daman responded, walking in behind Kat, so that she was sandwiched between the two men.

"Isn't it funny how fate works," he whispered in her ear. This wasn't the Daman she was used to.

Daman slowly ran his hands up her bare back, pausing to kiss the nape of her neck. Sergei pulled the straps of her gown down around her shoulders and bent his head to lick each of her nipples. They hardened from the warmth of his breath and the cold of the secret room. Kat had goosebumps all over her body, partly from the temperature of the room and from the excitement and anticipation of the two men kissing her.

Sergei grabbed her breast and kissed her roughly on the lips, while Daman continued kissing and nipping at the nape of her neck. She gasped and reached one arm over her head to hold Daman around the neck, and slipped her other arm around Sergei's waist, arching her body towards his.

Sergei grabbed her ass and held it tightly, and on the back of his hand he could feel Daman's cock straining at his pants. Sergei started rubbing Kat's ass vigorously and Daman pressed himself against Sergei's hand. Sergei took this as a cue and met Daman's lips with his over Kat's shoulder.

Kat found herself wetter than she'd been in her entire life. Here were the two men in her life embracing her and each other. She bit at Sergei's neck while he was deeply kissing Daman. She slid down in between their two bodies and pulled at the button on Sergei's tuxedo pants, letting his cock spring free. *No underwear, classic Sergei.* She quickly took Sergei's manhood in her mouth in one breath. She heard him groan into Daman's mouth as she took as much of his cock as she could into her mouth. She then turned and freed Daman's throbbing member. She licked up and down his shaft before also taking him fully in her mouth, while Sergei's throbbing cock sat rested on her shoulder.

Suddenly, Daman could take no more. In one move, he pulled Kat up from her knees, grabbing frantically at the hem of her gown and pulling it up over her head. He pushed aside her black lace panties and thrust into her causing her to inhale sharply. He held her hips, slowly increasing the tempo of his thrusting. As Daman continued his hard thrusts, Kat grabbed onto Sergei's hips and took his manhood in her mouth. Using the rhythm of Daman's thrusting, she sucked and deep throated Sergei.

"Slow down, Tigress. I don't want to come yet," Sergei gasped.

"Are you comfortable, sweetheart?" Daman asked.

"I wouldn't mind lying down."

Kat took both men by their hands and led them to a large velvet couch.

"Relax, my beautiful Queen," Sergei said, as he pushed her gently down onto her back. He began to kiss up and down her taut abs, finally pulling off her panties. Kat felt his warm breath between her legs, and this time, she was ready for the intense pleasure. He placed his whole mouth over her, and sucked slowly on each lip before delving into a light, flickering licking rhythm, breaking the pattern to suck hard on her clit.

Meanwhile, Daman gently straddled Kat's face, and she kissed his balls before taking them into her mouth and sucking on them hard. She felt him shiver. She reached up to guide his throbbing cock into her mouth. The three of them stayed that way, writhing and sucking and moaning, until the sensations overcame Kat. She arched her back and moaned and screamed around Daman's cock as the warmth from her body shot to her clit, sending her into a shuddering orgasm.

Sergei kissed her tummy and smiled up at her, his face covered in her wetness. He crawled up her body, slipping his hard cock into her wet slit. Daman turned and kissed Sergei, as Kat adjusted her angle so that she could continue sucking on Daman. To any onlooker, they would have looked like a writhing triangle of pleasure. Daman carefully lifted his body off Kat's face, and pulled his cock out of her mouth. Wordlessly, he pushed Kat onto her side, pausing to spread her wetness over his cock, before gently sliding it into her ass. Kat had never experienced such a strong sensation. She didn't feel dirty like she'd thought she would—she felt exhilarated and full. She loved the sensation and kissed Sergei hard on the mouth, as both Daman and Sergei slowly took turns thrusting into her. It felt extremely sensual, and waves of pleasure began to travel up and down her body. Sergei started pumping into her faster and faster, before suddenly grabbing onto Daman's ass as he bucked and filled her with his seed. This seemed to set Daman off, and he in turn grabbed Sergei's ass so that Kat was solidly sandwiched between the two of them. Daman grunted and seemed to growl as she felt him come inside her ass.

Afterwards, they lay there on the couch, panting, tangled in their post-orgasmic haze.

The three of them fell asleep on the couch, tucked under a fur blanket in the light of the crackling fire—Daman in the back and Sergei in the front. Kat felt as though a powerful demon of lust had taken over her body and there was no going back. She had given herself fully to both Daman and Sergei, finally admitting to herself that she'd fallen for both men equally. It was easy to forgive Sergei, he'd been acting out of jealousy and nothing more. If she were in his position, she knew she would have done the same.

And it was also hard to stay mad at someone who was tickling you and biting your back.

12

The three were roused abruptly by bright flashlights.

"Oh, my lord," exclaimed Natalia. She placed one hand on her forehead before falling backwards and fainting in her husband's arms.

"Mother!" shouted Kat, while clutching at the fur blanket. Daman and Sergei jumped behind the couch, desperately trying to find their discarded suits.

"Quickly, Katerina, help me get your mother onto the couch. We need to get her a glass of cold water for when she wakes up."

"I'll get it," Daman offered kindly. He'd located his pants and dress shirt and was now running out of the room and up the stairs, barefoot.

"I don't know what to say," Kat said. "Is she going to be okay? I feel so badly that she had to find out this way. Papa, what do I do?"

"It's going to be alright. Your mother just had a fainting spell. I suppose it surprised her to see you, um, well, see you the way, well…" He sputtered, unable to form a complete sentence.

"Father," Kat pleaded, as tears streamed down her face.

"It's okay, child, your mother will make sense of everything in time. For now, we need to be there for her when she wakes up. Where is Daman with the water?"

"How did you know his name?" Kat asked, puzzled.

Her father said nothing, so Kat continued, "I'm in love with him."

Sergei cleared his throat behind her. Now was as good a time as any, she realized, before bravely continuing. "Actually, I'm in love with Sergei too."

"Kat, this doesn't surprise me at all. Both of these boys are special, I know them both."

"But how?"

Her father sighed, "I have been dreading this day. The day that I have to reveal my secret life to my daughter."

"Dominic, Daman is taking way too long to come back" Sergei said, worriedly.

"Dominic?" Kat said, confused. "Dominic?"

Then all the puzzle pieces seemed to fall into place. *Her father was a shifter!*

"Yes, child." Your mother and I have learned that you have the gene that attracts shifters to you. Sergei was the only royal tiger shifter we could find that would satisfy your subconscious desire for a shifter, and satisfy our families' obligation to continue a strong blood-line. Your mother is starting to stir, and she will be fine. Come back when you've found Daman and that water. You go too, Sergei."

Sergei nodded and bowed to her father before darting through the passageway, following Kat. They ran into the now deserted hallway and, deciding it was better to stick together, headed towards the ballroom. If Daman had come looking for water, he would have surely tried the buffet table. At least, they hoped that's where he would be.

As they entered the ballroom, Sergei reached out and laced his fingers through hers. "We're going to find him," he said. "I'm sure everything's fine and he's just hiding somewhere, nervous to face your mother."

"Do you really think he's hiding right now?" she asked. "It's been almost an hour. Something is definitely wrong."

"Do you think he would have gone out to the courtyard or the garden to, you know, clear his mind?"

"Oh no," she said, her hand flying up to her mouth. "There's new guards on duty tonight—a group that I don't know very well."

"And I'm guessing they wouldn't hesitate to shoot a Siberian tiger on sight," he said, a look of concern coming over his face.

In the distance, they heard a single gunshot. A few of the party guests turned, but most of them just ignored it. They knew they were safe, every last one of them.

"You guessed right," she said, her hand flying to her mouth. "Come, before it's too late!" She grabbed him by the wrist and ran out of the ballroom.

They leapt down staircase after staircase until they were on the first floor. The pair burst through a pair of double glass doors, practically shattering the panes from the force of their bodies.

"Stop!" she shrieked when she saw a guard aiming at a dark figure, clearly wounded and limping to the edge of the forest. "Stop! He's my pet!"

"Your pet?" Sergei smirked.

Kat shot him the dirtiest look.

The guards lowered their guns, but kept them cocked. Kat ran towards the lump, which was moaning in pain. As they got closer, their worst fears were confirmed. It was Daman alright, and he'd been shot. Kat patted his fur all over, trying to feel for a bullet hole. She found nothing on his flanks or neck, which was a good sign.

"I found it," Sergei said. "It's in his leg. Can you change back, boy? I know it hurts, but it might ease the pain a bit."

Daman just growled and tried to bite Sergei.

"Okay, I was only asking. Listen Kat, we need to get him inside."

Sergei let out two sharp yelps, calling for her father.

"But how do we move him?" cried Kat.

They didn't need to worry long, as not even ten seconds later, Kat's father was by their side. He'd started running towards the treeline the minute he heard the gunshot.

He had a medical kit on him at all times, strapped around his waist in a leather pouch. With a pair of enormous tweezers, he proceeded to search for the bullet in the wound.

"It won't work, there's too much fur. I need scissors," he said gravely, reaching for a pair in his bag.

Kat couldn't watch. She turned around and held her body, giving into a fresh flow of hot tears. She was terrified that Daman had lost too much blood.

"There isn't a bullet, it just barely grazed his leg. All he needs is some stitches and he should be good to go."

"You hear that, you big crybaby? All you need is stitches," Sergei joked. Daman wasn't in the mood for jokes so he reached out and tried to bite Sergei's hand.

"Careful, I don't want to have to give both of you stitches. I only have enough for one wound."

Sergei rolled his eyes and walked over to Kat. He held her from behind, rocking her gently back and forth in the tall grass. Though she felt comforted from Sergei's touch, she hated the sound of the scissor work behind her. It was also strange that she was quite literally caught between worlds. On one side was the forest, which was dark and mysterious, with a musty, earthy smell. On the other side lay the bright square of grass and behind it, the palace brightly lit with golden lights. She could see some of the party guests through the windows. They wore enormous masks and some even wore wings. It reminded her of the night she'd snuck out and met Daman for the first time.

"Daman," she whispered. Sergei leaned into her and kissed the top of her head.

"He's going to be okay," he murmured into her hair. "We all are."

"How can you be so sure?"

"You heard what your father, our tiger leader, said earlier. Everything will sort itself out. Even if there are three of us, I don't think that's such a bad thing."

"I already made up my mind," she said firmly. "I'm not going anywhere without you both by my side."

He smiled and whispered in her ear, "That's what I was hoping you'd say."

Five minutes later Daman's wound was cleaned and expertly stitched. When they turned around, they saw that he had returned to his human form. He was sitting on the ground with his head in his hands, wrapped in a blanket, waiting for the medication to kick in.

"Glad you're alright, Daman. What should we do now?" Sergei asked.

"Let's head back to the palace. I'm exhausted, and we could all use some sleep, and something to eat," said Kat.

"And something strong to drink," Daman added. His leg was starting to feel comfortably numb and he found he could stand up again, with the assistance of his friends.

"Father, how are we ever going to thank you for everything you've done for us? You're the most incredible being I've ever met in my whole life," Kat said. She walked up to him and planted a kiss on his cheek.

"You're my daughter, I've protected you all my life. These two men are now stepping into that role" he said, bowing low. "I'm heading back home now but if you need anything don't hesitate to call for me." And with that he disappeared into the night.

As they walked down the hallway, they saw her mother was back at the party and laughing with her friends.

"I should get back home," Daman said.

"Absolutely not," Kat said. "You can both sleep here. I no longer care what my mother thinks. I know she seems uptight and opinionated on the outside, but she married my father, a shifter, so there's a reasonable woman in there, somewhere. Maybe I'm a little bit more like her than I thought." Kat mused.

"You don't have to tell us twice," Sergei joked.

"Hey, I'm not nearly as bad as my mother. At least I haven't shot either of you on sight."

"I definitely thought you were going to shoot me when you first met me," Sergei said.

"And I thought you were going to shoot him when you caught him with Olysia," Daman added.

She sighed. "Okay, fine. Maybe I'm a little bit untraditional when it comes to my emotions. Besides, you two are the exact same way. If it weren't for your feelings, we wouldn't be in this mess."

"The lady has a point," Daman said.

They reached Sergei's room and Kat opened the door for him. The bed had been made earlier, and the small lamp by his bed had been left on, bathing the room in a soft orange glow. They hoisted Daman into the bed and covered him with a thin blanket, before saying goodnight to each other.

"I feel like a small child," Daman complained.

"That's because you are," Sergei responded. "Come on man, a bullet grazed your leg and you practically fell apart! If a bullet grazed my leg, I'd be running and jumping like a regular person ought to."

"Sergei, you're not a regular person. Now please, get some sleep already. I'll see you two in the morning," Kat said.

"Goodnight," they responded in unison.

With lead feet, Kat shuffled towards her bedroom. She felt as though her body were made of iron, sinking further to the floor with each step.

That night, Sergei and Daman slept solidly, while Kat tossed and turned, consumed by strange dreams about precious stones and crystals. Each dream was another segment from her childhood, including the break-in at the palace. With sudden realization, she awoke confused. Could it be true? The tiger she saw all those years ago had been her father. There were times she was sure she was being watched. She sat up with the sudden realization that it had been her father, watching over her.

13

The next morning, at breakfast, Natalia was in an uncharacteristically quiet mood. Hungover from the night before, she wore large sunglasses to shield her eyes from the glare of the morning sun.

As soon as Kat sat down at the table, Natalia removed the sunglasses, revealing a stern look.

"Kat, I've had enough. You *will* be getting married," she stated.

Kat tossed back her head and laughed. "Mama, the only way I'm getting married is if I can marry two men, and last I checked that wasn't legal here."

"And do you think that the Emerald family is subject to such laws?"

"We are, aren't we?," Kat stammered, unsure of what to think.

"Pish! It seems we have a wedding to plan—a rather unique wedding that will go down in Russian history." And Kat's mother smiled the most genuine smile that Kat had ever seen on her cold face.

On the day of her wedding, Kat finally allowed her mother to pin her hair up.

"You look stunning," murmured Natalia in approval, as she inserted the last bobby pin. She had attached small orange and white gems to the bun, leaving two ringlets of blonde hair cascading down Kat's face.

"Do you really think so?" Kat asked, nervous.

"Kat, you look more beautiful than ever. And I'm sure both grooms will agree."

When it was time, Natalia kissed Kat on both cheeks, and brushed a tear from her eye. As she left to take her place in the garden, Kat looked in the mirror one last time, and smiled a knowing smile.

Outside, a soft orchestral melody began to float through the air. Kat floated down a rose-covered aisle, with her father next to her. As she reached the rose adorned trellis, he tenderly kissed her on the cheek, before presenting her to her grooms, nodding twice in approval.

They were officially wed in the middle of the day, seconds before a huge rainstorm. Right after Kat said her vows, the heavens seemed to open, dumping water on all the guests.

Kat thought it was hilarious. Instead of taking it as a bad omen, she took it as a sign from Beatrice. Although Dante was of a different faith and from a different country than Kat, she would never forget the nights she had prayed to the fictional angel Beatrice, hoping that one day she would fall madly in love with someone who would respect and care for her as much as Dante. Kat knew she was lucky, for she had not only been granted her prayer once, but twice, as she had found her Dante in both Sergei and Daman.

As the sky turned from grey to black and the rain continued its steady downpour, everyone rushed into the main ballroom to stay dry. The servants had chilled vodka shots waiting for guests at the door, as was tradition.

Daman felt as though he was the luckiest man alive. He would get to live out his life with his two best friends, and he finally had a place to call home. After spending weeks in that disgusting apartment, it felt amazing to sleep on white linen sheets and king-sized beds. Even though he still felt the call of the wild, he had begun to appreciate domesticity.

Sergei told him that it wouldn't last. He'd been living as a half-human all his life, and he found the only way to survive it was to hunt every so often in the forest. It was really the only way he kept his sanity.

The party guests continued drinking and dining long into the night, and Kat felt the need to escape the noise, if only for a little while. Natalia had planned the nuptials to take place on the eve of Kat's birthday. She would only be twenty for a few more hours, and she wanted to enjoy every second of it. Starting tomorrow, she would have to start attending to issues regarding the estate and their businesses and holdings, leaving her adventures with Sergei and Daman in the past. But today, she was a young, happy newlywed and wanted revel in the moment.

"So, my darling, when's the honeymoon?" Sergei growled in a low, seductive voice.

"We're living large. Do you really need a vacation from a vacation?" Daman teased.

"I was just thinking that the three of us should spend some quality time together," he said, winking.

"Let's start now!" Kat squealed and, lifting the hem of her dress, ran up the stairs toward her wing. The men glanced once at each other, then tossed their shot glasses over their shoulders, laughing, before sprinting up the stairs to join their Queen.

They were both husbands and Kings, and they were home.

ABOUT THE AUTHOR

AJ Wynter has been a romance ghostwriter for years, and has finally stepped out of the shadows! Bad boys are her thing; although hers usually have a heart of gold under a rough, tough, and probably bearded, exterior.

AJ is a proud feminist and does her best to craft strong and intelligent leading lady characters to square off against these bad boys.

When she's not writing, AJ spends her time reading and gardening at her off-grid cabin in the Canadian mountains.

www.ajwynter.com

www.facebook.com/author.aj.wynter

www.instagram.com/author_aj_wynter

20334745R00041

Printed in Great Britain
by Amazon